Heaven On Your Doorstep

Also by the same author

HALFWAY TO HEAVEN

Heaven On Your Doorstep

Max Sinclair

with
Carolyn Armitage

HODDER AND STOUGHTON
LONDON SYDNEY AUCKLAND TORONTO

Some names and situations in this story have been
disguised to protect the privacy of those involved.

British Library Cataloguing in Publication Data

Sinclair, Max
   Heaven on your doorstep.—(Hodder
   Christian paperbacks)
   1. Family — Religious life
   I. Title   II. Armitage, Carolyn
   261.8′3585   BV4526.2

  ISBN 0 340 39125 1

*Printed in Great Britain for Hodder and Stoughton Limited, Mill Road,
Dunton Green, Sevenoaks, Kent by Cox & Wyman Ltd., Reading
Hodder and Stoughton Editorial Office: 47 Bedford Square, London
WC18 3DP*

INTRODUCTION

We were walking hand in hand down the winding country
lane near our home. The evening summer sun was still
warm and the hedgerows smelled of sweet honeysuckle.

'This is just like heaven' Susie remarked, summing up
our feelings in that moment. I knew she was talking about
our togetherness rather than the beauty of our surround-
ings.

We met when we were fifteen. We are now forty, and this
book is the story of our relationship. It has not always been
heaven and still isn't at times! I have shared some of our
many failures as well as the good times.

The Bible is full of real-life people – warts and all! God
must have allowed us to know about their failures so that
we can avoid their mistakes, just as their good points can
also be an example to us. But the real aim of it all is that we
see how good God is, *whatever* we are like.

So this is not an expert handbook but a true story. My
aim is not to convince you that your experience should
conform to ours in every detail, but I am utterly committed
to the patterns, advice and directives of God's Handbook
for Life. I believe that whatever our situation, our God is
able to help us move towards experiencing something of
the delights of heaven on earth in our family relationships.

Good relationships are a taste of heaven. I believe this
'bit of heaven' is on our doorstep, but all too often we keep
the door shut or fail to open it wide.

1

It was my wedding-day.

I took a moment to remember this important fact as I squinted at my watch that morning and registered the early hour of 6.30 a.m. Then, with a start, I was fully awake and jumping out of bed to fling open the bedroom window and take some deep breaths of the scented September air.

I was marrying Susie today. 'Yippee,' I burst out suddenly to the quiet and unconcerned countryside.

Behind me in the bedroom, my Moss Bros. morning-suit was hanging on the door of the wardrobe. I looked at my watch again. It was far too early to dress, so I sat down on the bed and contemplated the suit. Black jacket with imposing tails, smartly striped trousers that had seemed ridiculously baggy when I had tried them on in the shop.

'They're fine, sir,' the assistant had told me patiently. 'They're meant to be like that.' Staring at my reflection in the mirror, I had thought I looked old fashioned and uncomfortable.

I sat up straight on the bed and squared my shoulders in anticipation of trying to cut a fine figure as the groom, only to be interrupted by my brother Bernard coming purposefully into the room.

I deflated my chest. 'Just practising,' I explained, and nodded in the direction of the suit. Bernard grinned.

'A perfect fit,' he pronounced appreciatively, stepping over to the wardrobe to remove a bit of imaginary fluff from the immaculate jacket. 'Very smart indeed.'

I was still doubtful.

'You'll look fine,' Bernard reassured me, 'so stop worrying. Just enjoy wearing it – there won't be many other such opportunities after all.'

Sheer joy at the prospect of the day burst through me again, and the niggles of concern about the formal etiquette of the occasion melted away – for the moment at least. I pulled on my dressing-gown and tripped over my shiny black wedding shoes as I followed Bernard downstairs.

We'd agreed we should have a hearty breakfast. Bacon, eggs, toast, coffee – the lot.

'Can't have you fainting in the service,' Bernard had said. I couldn't remember ever having fainted in my life, but it was a tribute to my brother's organisational talents and thoughtful concern for me that he took his duties as best man so seriously.

We sat in comfortable silence at the breakfast-table in the stone-flagged farmhouse kitchen, for all the world like our two younger selves stoking up on Mum's liberal helpings before racing out with our fishing-rods or swimming things or with wellingtons on to spend absorbing and happy hours by the river.

The farm had been a childhood paradise for us both. We had never needed to be coaxed outside for some fresh air – we loved the wide, open spaces and the endless variety of places to play and to lose ourselves. We especially loved getting our wellies full of water in the river! As we got older we were naturally drawn into all the busy activity of a mixed farm, and the school holidays were cheerfully taken up with milking cows, mending fences, driving tractors or looking after the sheep. It was my particular job to take charge of the orphan lambs, and every year I'd develop a real soft spot for the little creatures who totally depended on me for their food and well-being.

I felt a twinge of nostalgia at the thought of leaving the Sussex farm that had been my home for seventeen years. I was glad Sue loved the country too. We could plan lots of expeditions together, taking picnics to remote spots and sharing our enjoyment of God's beautiful creation.

I glanced at my watch once more, checking the date and the hour for the umpteenth time. What might Sue be doing right now? Her eyes would surely be sparkling with excitement, her smile broad and happy. I imagined her among billows of white fabric and lace and wondered what her dress would be like.

'Don't forget to stand up straight and put your shoulders back,' instructed my father as we prepared to leave. There was always a word of practical advice from Dad and suddenly the solemnity of the occasion impressed itself upon me once again.

'How do I look?' I asked. Dad, splendidly dressed himself, looked me up and down and nodded approvingly. 'Fine, son. Just fine.'

Bernard reappeared at the bedroom door. 'Come on, Max. We'll be late.' He strode across the room to the suitcase and snapped the lid shut. 'Are you ready?'

One last glance in the mirror, a flick at my grey top-hat like I'd seen Fred Astaire do in the films and I was on my way, determined to enjoy the day.

It wasn't far to St Leonard's, Sue's parish church, and to my relief we were in good time. The sun was shining warmly, performing its wedding-day duty to perfection, and Bernard and I hovered in the church porch for a few minutes welcoming early guests. I watched the approach to the church expectantly for one particular person, and at last her familiar figure came into view. The next moment my mother was hugging me and smiling her greeting.

'A lovely day,' she murmured, absently putting her hand up to the very pretty hat she was wearing. 'Is your father inside?'

I nodded, feeling her nervousness and wishing I could do something to ease the situation. She and my father had separated about the time Sue and I got engaged and the divorce was now going through. I'd been saddened and puzzled, but felt I understood a little better now. I wanted

9

to say how glad I was that they had both come, and how much I appreciated their willingness to put aside their differences for the wedding.

'It's lovely to see you,' I began, but Mum was already turning towards the church door and with a last squeeze of my hand she slipped inside.

'Let's go then, shall we?' Bernard prompted, and I followed him into the cool interior of St Leonard's. It was a modern, light church with a fascinating pulpit shaped like the bows of a boat. Somehow it didn't seem at all out of place in a seaside town. I'd been to services here several times with Sue and her parents, but for all its familiarity the church had a solemn feel about it that morning. I couldn't quite grasp that everyone was gathering in Sue's and my honour. The service, the beautiful flowers, the smiles of welcome – they were all just for us.

I looked anxiously towards Mum and Dad as we passed their pew. They were sitting stiffly together, and I imagined how they must be feeling. I gave them a hopeful grin, and to my relief they both smiled back cheerfully enough.

Once I'd sat down in my place at the front, my nerves got the better of me. Frantically, I tried to remember what I had to do and to my horror found that my mind was a complete blank. Behind me, the church was filling up and I listened to the rustles and footsteps and occasional murmur of voices with growing panic. How dreadful it would be to get anything wrong in front of all those people! I stared fixedly at the altar, glad that whoever wrote the rules for weddings had given the groom this moment's pause before the proceedings began. Surely I'd remember everything when the time came.

The organ music changed to announce Susie's arrival and Bernard nudged me. Tingles of excitement only seemed to make my nervousness worse, and I straightened my shoulders in almost instinctive recollection of Dad's advice as I stood up on rather shaky legs.

'Don't forget what I said,' Bernard whispered urgently

at my side. 'When you see Sue's white dress, that's the moment to step out beside her.'

I nodded, relieved that my brother seemed in excellent control of what was going on. I waited for several seconds until I was sure Sue would be nearing the front of the church and then peered out of the corner of my eye for sight of her dress. There it was. Time to go. I stepped boldly out of the pew straight into the path of the vicar in his white surplice.

It was a terrible moment. I stood frozen to the spot, utterly taken aback. Then the vicar, Geoffrey Shaw, caught my eye, his amusement evident, and suddenly the spell was broken. The awesomeness of the occasion lost its hold on me and instead I wanted to join the vicar in a good laugh. We both retained our composure, however, and I stepped back quickly to let him pass, making sure that the vision in white behind him really was my bride before I took my place beside her.

Sue looked breathtakingly lovely. As we stood together facing the altar, I could hardly believe this long-awaited moment had really arrived. We exchanged our vows solemnly and fervently, eyes locked together, a shy smile on Sue's lips.

'Magnify the Lord with me,' read Tom Rees, my uncle, from Psalm 34, his voice ringing through the church, drawing everyone into its embrace, 'and let us exalt his name together.' Oh yes, Lord, I echoed silently. Let that be true in our marriage.

Sue's uncle led the prayers. 'May Max and Sue's home be happy, and bring glory to your name.' 'Amen,' confirmed the congregation, and again I lifted my heart to God in a sincere desire to see those words become reality.

The organ thundered out the last hymn and we joined in with every ounce of our being.

'We rest on thee, our shield and our defender . . .'

I looked at Sue beside me and swelled with happiness. We would be together for better or worse, and right then there was nothing else I wanted in the whole world.

'We go not forth alone ... strong in thy strength ... in thy name we go.' It meant everything that God was with us. He had brought us together and led us this far, and His presence seemed to set the seal on our future happiness. He was the security on which we built our hopes and dreams. 'We go in faith,' we sang, 'our own great weakness feeling, and needing more each day thy grace to know.' Perhaps those words were passed over too quickly. Perhaps I should have been more aware that blissful day of our natural human weakness and should have been more earnest in acknowledging our need of God's grace. But we were lost in our love for each other, and nothing could jolt our boundless, joyful confidence in our future together.

I had never doubted that we were right for each other. My certainty stemmed from years previously when I had innocently asked Mum, 'How do you know who to marry?' I was 10 and it was bedtime. Mum was busily tucking in the bedclothes and my father was standing by the window. I remember hearing him clear his throat as he often did before saying something important.

'That's a very good question, Maxim,' he said, while Mum continued to pat the bedclothes. I waited expectantly.

'The most important thing is to marry a real Christian.'

I was instantly satisfied by his answer. So that was how you knew! Contentedly, I snuggled under the sheets.

Then Mum added, 'Well, that's the most important thing, but it's probably also good to marry someone from the same sort of family who is interested in the same kind of things as you.'

This was more puzzling. I didn't know what other sort of families there were, and couldn't think of any girls I'd met who were interested in fishing or tractors. But I was happy to know a little bit more about such an important subject and slept soundly, dreaming of catching a ten-pound trout in our river.

Later, when I was at school, I was given a further piece of advice. Our Christian Union speaker told us we should pray from time to time about the person we might marry. 'Pray for God's help in making the right decision.' Any prospect of marriage seemed a long way off for a bunch of teenagers, but I was impressed by his words and occasionally prayed as he advised.

Such gems of wisdom were far from my mind when I first met Sue, and even as we spent more time together and got to know each other better, thoughts of marriage never seriously preoccupied me. Life was always too full.

On a Scripture Union beach mission in the summer of 1964 we realised our friendship was developing into something special. We were part of a team of twenty, running a hectic two-week programme on a Sussex beach. From dawn till dusk we were planning treasure hunts and games for the children, building enormous sand-castles and competing to see whose would last the longest as the tide came in and the waves undermined all our hard work. We sang choruses during the daily informal service round the sand pulpit and tried with a thousand ingenious visual aids to communicate a living Christian faith to the youngsters and their parents. It was exhausting, exhilarating work. Sue and I teamed up to help lead the singing, with me strumming away on my guitar, and we practised and prayed together regularly. We both believed God could use this holiday to touch the hearts of those we spoke to, and were thrilled when someone responded by wanting to hear more about Christ or take a new step of faith.

Our common concern to share what God had done for us and could do for others drew us closer together and forged a strong and significant link between us. Shyly, on a rare free afternoon, we recognised how much our friendship meant to each of us, but we didn't dare wonder openly about our possible future.

Sue was more quickly certain about this than I was, but when I seemed engrossed in my university studies and then arranged a skiing holiday the following Christmas instead of choosing to spend time with her, she began to wonder if our paths were drawing close after all. Perhaps God had something else in store.

'You know,' she confided on the one evening we spent together before the university term began in the New Year, 'lots of my family have been missionaries.' I was driving her home in my father's car after a hilarious couple of hours ice-skating with friends at the Queensway rink in London. It was the first time we'd seen each other since the beach mission.

'I sometimes think that's what I'll be doing before long.'

I was quite unprepared for such a turn in the conversation. Sue had never volunteered her long-term plans and dreams, and what she was saying now seemed disconcertingly far from my own tentative thinking about our future. For an alarming moment I saw Sue outside a mud hut in Africa while I would probably be jumping off a commuter train in the City of London. The two images were so incongruous I almost laughed, but Sue was in deadly earnest. She launched into various colourful descriptions of missionary life, which usefully prevented me from having to say anything.

'You could never say a missionary's life is a dull one, could you?' she prompted eventually. I shook my head. 'And there must be nothing more fulfilling than working for the Lord where He wants you to be.' Sue's voice trailed away and she turned to look out of the car window.

My thoughts were racing. I didn't know about Sue's concerted praying and longing for God to clarify what was happening between us. The evening we'd just spent together had confirmed how much she meant to me, but I still felt we were really too young to let things develop too fast or too seriously. We were both only 19. Even though I sensed Sue was needing some kind of reassurance, I couldn't bring myself to voice what I was only just admitting to myself. I murmured something about not being sure that the mission field was necessarily her calling and then lapsed into silence, appearing to concentrate hard on the road. Poor Susie must have been more mystified than ever.

There wasn't a sudden moment of decision. I hadn't spent much time trying to decide what qualities I might hope to find in the girl of my dreams, nor had I got to the point of working out how I should know someone was right for me, or I was right for her. Marriage hadn't become a specific goal, but I knew I definitely did want to spend time with Sue the following holiday.

There are many different routes by which people travel towards each other and decide to get married. Background and circumstances influence events inevitably, and every couple will have their own story of how it happened. It's a fact of life that there is no blueprint, which simply serves to emphasise the richness and variety of God's creation. For Sue and me, marriage eventually became the logical extension of our friendship, and the foundation for that friendship to grow and blossom into something very precious indeed was laid that Easter with our 'spring charter'.

It was a step of commitment to each other, an agreement as to how we should conduct our relationship. We wanted to give ourselves a framework and a purpose, and submit ourselves consciously and together to God's leading.

We admitted to each other that one of the most important and precious aspects of our relationship was our closeness, and this was something we wanted not only to preserve but to increase. So we built into our charter the determination to be completely open and honest at all times. We would share everything. How else could trust be maintained? And without trust, how could any relationship endure? As Sheldon Vanauken writes of his relationship with Davy in his moving book, *A Severe Mercy*, 'Total sharing, we felt, was the ultimate secret of a love that would last for ever.' Like them, Sue and I wanted our trust in each other to be based not only on love and loyalty but on 'the fact of a thousand sharings, a thousand strands twisted into something unbreakable.'

At the same time, we knew this was just a beginning. We

had a long way to go before we could decide whether our security and confidence in one another was sufficient to sustain a lifetime's commitment. We still didn't mention the word 'marriage', knowing the relationship had to develop unhurriedly if its roots were to be deep and firm. The second point of our charter was that we should gladly seek to deepen our friendship, but not at the expense of everything else. There were other priorities in our lives, such as our studies, and these were to be maintained. We would not try to impose our wishes on the relationship, but let it develop in its own time.

We were very serious as we discussed these things, perhaps unusually so, but this was a measure of the importance we attached to the growing bond between us. Our mutual respect was already too great for either of us to be careless of the other's feelings, and even as we admitted how deep those feelings actually went we knew we had a responsibility not only to each other but also to God. We sought to be obedient to Him first and foremost and to this end the third part of our charter was agreed. We would not permit ourselves even the tiniest physical expression of our affection. The biblical mandate was clear: enjoyment of any sexual relationship was a privilege for marriage alone, in a setting where two people were permanently committed to each other. We wanted to honour God's command completely.

For us, this meant restraint even in areas which on the surface seemed perfectly innocent – holding hands, for instance, or kissing. We knew others didn't share our conviction and that many might say such expressions of love were perfectly legitimate. We certainly didn't believe that they were wrong in themselves, but we knew that physical closeness could develop into something disproportionately important, blocking the deeper communication we longed to have and believed was the proper foundation for an enduring relationship. We knew we were very human, and didn't want anything to weaken the special bond between us.

16

Our charter may have been solemn but there was no denying the excitement we both felt as we hammered it out. We were taking responsibility for our relationship and, at the same time, submitting its development to God's sovereign hand. The future seemed full of promise – but it was not to be all plain sailing from then on. For one thing, we were now much more consciously on the lookout for evidence that we could be happy together on a long-term basis – that we were, indeed, 'right' for each other.

The following summer I was a regular visitor to Sue's home and often enjoyed a game of tennis with her brother Simon. He was rather better than I, and usually clinched the game. One particularly hot afternoon, I plopped despondently into a chair in the Young's kitchen, while Sue busied herself preparing several glasses of orange juice. Simon had taken the set off me once again, and my spirits weren't helped by his striding through the kitchen on his way to the garden looking as fresh as if he'd just got up from a relaxed afternoon's snooze. He hardly paused to knock back his drink.

'Really enjoyed that game, Max,' he said warmly before disappearing. So had I, and said so. I certainly didn't mind losing, but there was something else that worried me. I stared glumly at Simon's retreating back.

'You look hot and bothered,' Sue said sympathetically, handing me my drink. She was inviting me to say what was on my mind.

'Mmm.' Silence while I took a sip of orange. Sue waited patiently.

'I have never seen your brother look anything else but fit, tanned and bursting with muscular energy,' I volunteered eventually. 'Well, and your father too, not to mention Andy.' Sue had two brothers and they both outclassed me completely when it came to sport. I had managed to scrape into the school tennis team but competitive sport didn't really interest me. Sue's father had played rugby for Scotland and was a Cambridge boxing blue.

'And here I am feeling like a wet dishcloth and ready to put my feet up,' I finished lamely. I grinned at her sheepishly and rather apologetically. Not only must I have sounded dreadfully petulant, but I hadn't even managed to be straight about what was really bothering me. Here we were, committed to being absolutely honest with each other, and I couldn't get very far towards confessing my feelings of inferiority. I certainly couldn't express my fear that I might not be measuring up to Sue's idea of what a man should be.

But the gentle look with which she greeted my words wasn't at all puzzled or distant.

'Muscles aren't everything, you know,' she said. 'And anyway,' as she got up from her chair and picked up her brother's empty orange glass from the sideboard, 'you're an interesting, mysterious sort of person and I love you.' The orange glass doubtless didn't appreciate the impact of these mind-blowing words, but I no longer cared a jot whether I was sportsman or dishcloth of the year. Sue had told me that it didn't matter.

Then there was the much more serious matter of my job. My intended career in accountancy was not one to which Sue found it easy to relate. Her father was a doctor and she and her family were inevitably involved in his work – what with the phone ringing and people calling and her father sometimes seeing patients at home. He was constantly in and out of the house. Sue couldn't imagine what it would be like to live with someone who was away for a prescribed number of hours every day, and often away mid-week, too, on visits to clients. The business world was a mystery to her, and it was going to be hard to gain a better insight into office life when she couldn't participate as she had done in her father's work.

'I wish he wasn't a City gent,' she confessed to her diary.

To me she simply said, 'It's all very different, but I'm sure I'll get used to it.' It was a step she was prepared to take towards me, and I was grateful for it. From the beginning of my training I tried to draw her into all that I

18

was doing so that she didn't feel cut off or threatened by an alien world.

'Hasn't she been to domestic science college?' my mother said when she knew things were getting serious between Sue and me.

'Mum, that just doesn't matter,' I said patiently.

'Well, if you're thinking of getting married you really ought to encourage her to go,' my mother insisted. 'How ever will she feed you?'

My father was worried about her lack of business sense. He judged business acumen and career prospects to be matters of the highest order, and was genuinely concerned that the woman who'd won my affections apparently had neither. It didn't seem the moment to tell him about Sue's interest in social work.

But they liked her. They liked her a lot, which rather surprised me at first since she so obviously seemed to fall down on some of the things they thought important. I was reassured by their affection for her. Also I knew Sue was full of practical common sense and seemed instinctively to know some of what the domestic science college might have taught her about homemaking and presenting a meal. I knew I could manage the bank statements and that she would be quite happy about that. We understood one another, enjoyed similar interests, and were relaxed in each other's company. Yet despite all that, I would have felt uneasy if my parents had harboured serious doubts. They knew me best after all. Their opinions mattered.

Dad had said more than once, 'The girl you marry must think you are the sun, moon and stars.' He never raised any objection about Sue on this count – perhaps he'd seen a look in her eyes!

By the summer of 1966, when Sue had completed two years of her English studies at Keele University and I had finished my degree, we knew without a doubt that we wanted to get married, but there was a serious question that we still needed to resolve. Was it really God's will that we should marry?

In one sense it seemed only natural that two people who were deeply in love should think about getting married, but we wanted to be sure that this was God's intention for us. Looking back, we could see how the bond between us had deepened and it seemed that God had blessed and confirmed our relationship. Wasn't this enough? Not quite.

As Christians, committed to living according to God's Word and seeking to be guided by Him at every step, we were already in harmony with the biblical command not to be 'yoked with unbelievers'. This injunction had come into focus for me as I'd contemplated the future with Sue – it simply made sense. How could two people whose fundamental beliefs and goals were radically different ever draw really close and be happy together? The Christian faith that Sue and I shared was a wonderful source of joy and security for us both, and without it our relationship would have been immeasurably weakened.

We asked ourselves nonetheless whether it was possible that we were just being selfish and wanting to enjoy our love for its own sake. Maybe God had given us this deep friendship for our encouragement and growth as individuals, and not for marriage. Neither of us was keen to contemplate such possibilities, but we determined to seek God for His specific enlightenment. We had faith that He would reassure us if we were on the right road, and in the deepest part of ourselves we knew that if marriage was not in His plan we should not only be wrong to ignore that, but inviting all sorts of problems if we did.

We studied the Bible, thought and talked a lot, and prayed.

We discovered in no uncertain terms that marriage was upheld in both the Old and New Testaments. It was God's idea, not man's invention. Hadn't He made Adam a companion because He saw that it was not good for him to be alone (Gen. 2: 18)? He didn't just approve of marriage – He created it. We were assured on that point, but did anything suggest He intended something different for us?

We tried to respond honestly to the question of whether

we could serve God better on our own.

'I suppose if I were single I could go and be a missionary or something, as I was thinking before.' Sue ventured as we talked soberly on one of our long walks. She sounded very doubtful.

'Whereas if you married me you'd have to waste time cooking meals and washing shirts you mean,' I teased, trying to coax laughter back into her eyes.

We agreed that there were lots of ways God could use us as a couple. Marriage would be a new and different sphere of service, but certainly not a lesser one. If anything, we saw greater opportunities ahead. It seemed confirmation of our rightness for each other that the future apart and on our own looked daunting and uncertain.

'The fact that you are there and support me means a lot,' I said carefully. 'I can be – well, myself more easily I suppose. Do things more wholeheartedly.'

Sue said it was exactly the same for her. 'I just can't imagine life without you.'

We were admitting our need for each other, but at the same time we saw that being together contributed to our wholeness as individuals and thus to our ability to be open and available to God. There seemed no obstacle to our stepping forward into marriage. Everything pointed in this direction, and there was really no other way we could go. We appreciated more than ever that our love was a precious gift from God to be gratefully received and enjoyed.

Then there was the question of timing. In July I was due to start work at a large firm of London accountants, earning the princely salary of £600 a year. We might just manage to live on that but we could not possibly afford to buy a house. Even renting somewhere would probably be a bigger drain on our resources than we could manage. Sue had another year to go at Keele and although it might be possible for her to go straight into a job once she graduated it was more likely that she would need to do some further training. Besides that, we didn't want to get ourselves into a position of relying too heavily on the income from any job Sue might take because we'd agreed that, once we were married, homemaking would be an important priority, not just for our own benefit but so that others could find a warm welcome and relaxation under our roof.

'We'll have to wait,' I concluded reluctantly. It looked as though we wouldn't be able to start out on our life together for more than two years.

Our patience quickly wore thin, but before many months had gone by we were given an unexpected and wonderful bonus. I couldn't wait to tell Sue what had happened, and drove up to Keele that October weekend hardly able to contain my excitement.

I found her on the floor of her room, surrounded by prospectuses for social-work courses.

'There are so many I really don't know which one to choose,' she lamented. 'And it's difficult anyway when my heart isn't in it.' She immediately looked abashed at such a confession and hurriedly assured me that she liked the look of some of the courses but was wondering whether teacher training might not be a better option.

'Mmm, difficult,' I said, playing for time. 'Tell you what – why don't we get married when you graduate, instead? That'll solve the problem!'

'What? You don't mean ... But I thought ...'

'Dad says he'll buy us a house.'

Sue's eyes were big and sparkling at any time, but now they were larger and brighter than ever.

'Oh Max, really? That's wonderful, that's *wonderful*, but didn't he think it was a better idea to wait until you'd qualified? Oh, I can't believe it!'

It was a marvellously generous gesture on my father's part, and characteristic of his concern that we should be financially secure. He gave us a start that we could hardly have dreamed of, but right then we were focusing on the immediate benefit – no more waiting. We could set the date.

There was the engagement ring of course, and the next

day we drove to Chester to join the throng of Saturday shoppers. We were weaving our way through the crowds looking for a jeweller when I stopped dead in my tracks. How could I have forgotten something so important? Sue looked thoroughly startled as I swung round and took both her hands in mine.

'Susie.'

'What's the matter?'

'Susie, will you marry me?'

There we were, heading off to buy an engagement ring and I hadn't even proposed properly, let alone been accepted.

She looked away for a few seconds, still holding my hands, and I quavered momentarily. What was she thinking?

Then she turned back and returned my gaze. 'Yes, I will,' she said definitely, and we threw our arms round each other, much to the surprise of the other shoppers jostling to pass us. We sheepishly released each other and tried to melt into the crowd farther down the pavement.

We chose a lovely antique emerald and diamond ring. It was just right, discreet and not too showy and matching Sue's hazel eyes. When it came to paying for it I discovered I had hardly any money on me so Sue paid.

Our feet were several inches above the pavement as we walked back to the car, and once we were inside I took the ring out of its case and slipped it on Susie's finger. She smiled her deep smile and we fell into each other's arms again.

'I'll have to do the honours with your father too you know,' I reminded her as we drove back to the university. 'Ask him for your hand, I mean.'

In our study of what the Bible says about marriage, we'd read the Genesis passage which says 'A man will leave his father and mother and be united to his wife, and they will become one flesh' (Gen. 2: 24). And we had seen that Paul repeats these words in his letter to the Ephesians when he is instructing them on the importance of love and respect

23

between marriage partners. 'Each one of you also,' Paul goes on to say, 'must love his wife as he loves himself, and the wife must respect her husband' (Eph. 5: 33). According to the Bible, once two people were married, loyalty to the parents took second place to loyalty to each other. I was therefore convinced I should ask Sue's father for his permission to marry her and take on the responsibility for her which had previously been his.

When it came to the moment, I threw myself into the task with vigour. I got down on bended knee and begged Dr Young for his daughter's hand in marriage.

'And what are your prospects, young man?' he enquired with mock severity.

'Well, sir, if I marry your daughter – wonderful. If not, pretty dreadful I'm afraid.'

'I see,' Dr Young scratched his beard in deliberation. Then he boomed over my head, 'Yes, take her away. I'll be more than happy for you to pay her expenses from now on.'

He burst into a hearty guffaw as I scrambled up from my humble position. I clasped his extended hand which was at least twice the size of mine, and was surprised and a little embarrassed to see tears on his cheeks even as he laughed.

'Delighted,' he was saying. 'Just delighted.'

I knew the tears were an expression of his deep feeling and sincere gladness. I remembered Sue on the Sunday evening of our engagement, when we'd gone to the little Baptist church at Newcastle-under-Lyme which she attended regularly. Throughout the service, tears had rolled silently down her cheeks. Something deep within her had been triggered by our worshipping together, and I now realised that her ability to express her feelings readily probably came from her father.

Sue's parents' approval set the seal on our decision, and all the more so because in the early days of our relationship they weren't sure that we were well suited. They were concerned about the differences in our temperaments. I was quieter and more thoughtful than their daughter, who lived life with an apparently boundless energy and was very open about what she thought. I didn't see such differences in character as a problem at all and decided we complemented each other rather than anything else, but it was good to know that the Youngs too were reassured. Sue and I were blissfully unaware of any potential difficulties in our partnership, and were far too much in love to have been put off by them anyway.

During our wedding service, I felt overwhelmingly filled and blessed by both God's love and Sue's love. We were on the edge of a new and exciting life, a life in which surely no obstacle could get in our way. I felt a better person with Sue. I loved to see her smiling and happy, and our hearts throbbed as one in a seemingly effortless beat.

I had no idea that to maintain such harmony might involve great effort.

2

I was brought down to earth with a bump only hours after the reception. It was a real blow to my pride to be lying stretched out on our double bed having my brow mopped by Sue when I should have been taking her tenderly into my arms. Our hotel meal in the evening had made me violently ill.

'You look awful,' Sue murmured sympathetically when I staggered out of the bathroom for the second time.

'The meat was definitely reheated,' I lamented.

'Go on,' Sue teased. 'I bet you ate too much at the reception,' and she leaned over the bed where I'd collapsed again to give me a loving hug.

Sue did all the driving the next day. I sat limply beside her, nursing a bottle of kaolin and morphine and praying that our hotel in Scotland would be an improvement on the rather dowdy one we'd just left. We had ten days ahead of us, and I'd imagined the whole thing would be a perfect time of blissful happiness. So far, my dream had not quite been realised.

We were heading for the little village of Rockcliffe in the south-west of the country, a beautiful and secluded spot that was near the farm where I'd spent the first five years of my life. As we rounded the last bend and turned into the drive of the Barons Craig Hotel, Sue gasped in admiration.

'Oh Max, it's perfect.'

Built of the grey-stone granite that was characteristic of the area, the hotel had a tower with turrets that made it look very romantic and almost like a castle. It overlooked the pretty Rockcliffe bay, and we could see the winding coastline and heather-covered hills stretching beyond it for what seemed miles. There was a thick pine forest climbing steeply behind.

Sue jumped out of the car and I followed more slowly. A huge archway dominated the porch, and the door was of solid oak. Sue squeezed my hand in delight as we stepped inside. No stale smell of beer and cigarettes this time, but a friendly, family atmosphere that made us feel instantly at home. Was it excitement or hunger pangs gnawing at my stomach? I felt very much better.

'Well, shall we go to the farm today or just explore round here first?' I asked as we flung open the curtains of our bedroom the next morning. My childhood haunts were just a few miles up the coast, and I was longing to share them with Sue. It was a beautiful day, and we leaned comfortably on the window-sill together, breathing the sea air and feasting our eyes on the view. The bay looked so inviting that we decided not to leave it so soon and opted for a swim after breakfast. Then we took a picnic through the forest to Kippford where we watched the little sailing-boats dotting in and out of the harbour.

Time stood still. We were quietly content in each other's company, full of love and of the beauty of Scotland. Our hands were clasped tightly together and every so often I looked down at them wonderingly. Their entwined closeness seemed to reflect our own closeness.

I remembered the very first time I'd taken Sue's hand. It was in Newcastle when I'd fought my way through a crowd of anxious students, all craning their necks to see if their names were pinned to the exam notice-board. After a moment's search, I found mine. I'd passed and got my degree. Exultant, I bounded out of the building and back to the car where Sue was waiting for me, and we drove straight out into the country for a celebratory walk. I knew another milestone had been passed, and as we walked together, hardly noticing the pouring rain, I slipped my hand into hers. It was a precious moment.

27

We had never regretted our spring charter and our strict self-discipline in all things physical. It had nurtured our commitment to each other, and prepared us for the sweetness of intimate love that we were now beginning to taste.

I'd often wondered before our wedding-night whether we should find our first experience of sexual intimacy difficult. I'd heard the 'experts' on television and radio extolling the virtues of sexual prowess, and implying that the early days of marriage would be vastly easier if the couple knew what they were doing. For Sue and me, the joys of discovering this new experience together far outweighed any difficulties, so that even without the biblical mandate we wouldn't have wanted to do anything differently. It didn't matter if we didn't make love expertly because we weren't trying to impress or pretend to each other. There was no shadowy past figure with whom either of us was being compared, and our commitment to each other meant that we should still be there in the morning and the next day and the next. There was a wonderful security that meant we could relax completely. And at moments of ignorance or embarrassment we were able to laugh. Our vulnerability together brought us closer. Our innocence actually cemented the relationship.

As those balmy honeymoon days succeeded one another, we saw clearly that our newly-discovered sexual relationship was simply and beautifully an extension of what we already had. It was a new and deeper dimension, but it wasn't something separate from what we'd enjoyed together so far. Nor was it the crowning glory of our relationship, casting everything else that we'd found precious into shadow. For us, our sharing together at every level continued to be as important as it had always been, and many years on I feel still more that marriage is primarily about a relationship and not sex. Our love-making was an expression of that sharing of all of ourselves with each other, and was therefore a deep joy and delight to us both.

We explored every inch of Rockcliffe and the surrounding coastline. Sue caught a glimpse of a deer in the forest one morning, and as we waited in breathless suspense on the narrow little path we were rewarded with the sight of rippling, tawny limbs flashing through the trees. We swam regularly and scrambled among the rocks along the coast. Some days we climbed the path up to Castle Point where we flopped on to the coarse grass and looked out to the islands in the estuary, along the River Urr to Kippford where the boats were tiny pinpoints on the water, and back in the other direction towards the Solway Firth and the peaks of the Lake District. It felt as though we were on top of the world. I looked down at the foaming water below, curling and crashing over the rocks where the river met the sea.

'It's like us,' I said to Sue. The wind was blowing her long brown hair across her face, and she shook it away in a characteristic gesture.

'What is?'

'The river.' I indicated the expanse of the estuary with my open hand. 'It's made up of different streams and yet it is itself with its own identity. And lots of rivers make up the sea but it has its own identity too.'

The image stayed clearly with me. We were the same as before, but different now we were a couple. We were ourselves, but more. All the elements of the streams were contained in the river, and the river in the sea, but each was larger, steadier, and a new entity in itself.

Before we left, we went to the tiny sandy bay where I used to play as a boy and peered into the pool which yielded crabs and shrimps in those long-ago days. We plodded across the beach towards the receding tide and I pointed out the nets strung between stakes in the shallows and told Sue how I used to follow the fishermen and watch fascinated as they scooped dozens of flounders out of the water. She listened, fascinated, and I got quite carried away reliving my memories for her. By the time we headed back for the hotel, I felt almost as if Sue had been with me during those early years. The memories were shared completely.

We couldn't believe how quickly the time sped by, and when the day of departure loomed we frantically arranged to extend our honeymoon by another week. It was unbearable to let go such happiness. We 'feasted on love', as C.S. Lewis put it, but it had to end sometime. When we eventually turned our backs on Rockcliffe it was with a heavy dread of all the old and new demands that awaited us back in London.

Our return was not made easier by the fact that the sale of the house we'd been trying to buy had fallen through just days before the wedding. We'd been gazumped. I hadn't bargained for carrying my new wife over the rather dingy threshold of my East Dulwich flat, especially when I knew she didn't like it much. I'd moved in when I started work in the City, and was so delighted to find anywhere at all that my letter to Sue only expressed jubilation at the convenience of being ten minutes from London Bridge by train. I didn't go into detail about its age or poor state of repair, nor did I describe the rather tatty decoration or mention the fact that there was no garden.

'Dulwich Park is only a few minutes' walk away and it's lovely,' I said brightly when she first came to visit. Like me, Sue preferred open spaces and fresh air to the bustle and grime of city life, and I'd detected a distinct lack of enthusiasm in her polite manner on that occasion.

Our new house was to have been in Orpington, still convenient for London but within easy reach of the rolling Kent countryside. My bachelor pad was rather an uninviting alternative, but it looked as if we were going to have to make the best of it.

The phone rang just minutes after we'd got back. I'd plonked the suitcases rather glumly on the floor and Sue had proposed a cup of restorative coffee and disappeared into the kitchen.

It was my father.

'Well, Max, I've been busy while you were away and I've got the house back.'

'What?' I couldn't believe it.

'The chap agreed to our offer in the end,' Dad went on, but further explanation was lost on me as I shouted the good news to Sue.

Dad's next words checked my elation.

'There's still a slight problem, I'm afraid. The woman won't move out, and until she does we're stuck. Legally, the contracts can't be exchanged. We'll just have to hope she has a change of heart before too long, otherwise it won't be worth our hanging on.'

Dad was marvellous at such negotiations. When he'd said he'd buy us a house he'd meant he would take care of every last detail, but this was a difficulty none of us had foreseen. We'd in fact intruded on a very sad situation. We were buying the house from a couple who were getting divorced and the husband had obviously put the house on the market without his wife's consent.

I replaced the telephone receiver slowly. Our hopes had been raised only to be dashed again, and our sympathy for the woman was tinged with our own regret at being denied our dream house. It had seemed perfect in every way, the home we'd longed for, and we'd thanked God from the bottom of our hearts when our offer had been accepted. It had been a real blow to learn that someone else had topped that offer, but it was a salutary lesson. Just because we trusted God to provide for our needs, it didn't mean we'd never have any disappointments. We'd fallen into the trap of thinking that everything would go smoothly if brought to God in prayer, and were in danger of confusing our own desires with God's plan for us. He might have something quite different in store.

At the same time we couldn't shake off the fact that the house had seemed right in so many ways. Even as we tried to reconcile ourselves to losing what we'd set our hearts on, we knew that God could remove the obstacles if indeed

31

it was part of His plan for us.

'It's in your hands,' we prayed. 'There's nothing we can do.'

Now here it was, held out to us again and yet tantalisingly beyond our reach.

'Perhaps we could go and talk to the woman,' Sue suggested hopefully. It seemed a reasonable idea. We surely couldn't lose anything by it, and in our naivety we presented ourselves at the front door the next day.

I don't think we went with the conscious intention of persuading her to give way, but perhaps we thought she might be sympathetic to what we saw as our plight. But we had no idea of her own desperate situation, and when she eventually let us in, we learned that she simply had nowhere else to go. Unless her husband found her somewhere to live or provided maintenance of some kind she would be homeless.

We were more than a little discouraged by the time we returned to the flat, not just because there was no easy solution to our own dilemma – which was nothing in comparison to what the poor divorcee was facing – but because such unhappiness could exist in a world which had seemed quite unspoilt and full of promise just a few days before. How could a relationship that must have begun in hope and gladness go so terribly sour?

We waited, and half-looked for another place to buy. Then we heard our dream house had been vacated. It seemed it was to be our home after all.

'Oh, I do hope she has found somewhere nice to live,' was Sue's immediate reaction, voicing my own thoughts.

Once the contracts were exchanged, everything went through very quickly and in three weeks we were packing up the flat. Now we would have our own home. Sue had done her best to brighten the old place by cleaning and polishing and filling it with flowers, but it wasn't the same as somewhere of our very own and we could hardly wait to move. We were also desperate for a garden – every inch of Dulwich Park had been explored by the time we left.

We called our new home Rowan Cottage. It wasn't really a cottage, but it had a pinkish wash over the outside walls and diamond-paned windows so it looked a bit like one, and there were two red-berried rowan trees outside the front door. It was part of an estate of small detached houses built just before the Second World War, and set among quiet, tree-lined roads. Best of all, it had a garden that was hopelessly overgrown but full of exciting potential. Our hearts overflowed with gratitude to God and for my father's generosity.

There was masses we had to do to get the inside of the house straight. On the first evening we stood in the living-room and wrinkled our noses at the ugly ceramic tiles that surrounded the empty fireplace.

'That would look so much better with red bricks around it, and a warm, coloured rug on the floor in front of the hearth.' My voice echoed round the empty room.

'*Much* better,' agreed Sue enthusiastically. 'We could polish these floorboards and paint the walls a lighter colour.'

'And choose warm shades for the furnishings if this is going to be a room to relax in.'

We bounced ideas around and threw dreams into the air, thrilled that we agreed on what was needed and eager to get down to the scrubbing and painting.

Gradually, our days settled into a pattern. We began them very differently, and this was something we had to get used to from the start. Sue would wake up and be ready at once to jump out of bed and busy herself with a hundred and one activities, whereas I needed more time to collect myself and preferably sip a cup of coffee before I could respond with any sense and civility to the waking world. At first Sue would talk eagerly about something she'd been thinking or forgotten to tell me, but she soon noticed my sleepy lack of reaction and wisely decided on a different approach. I was left to surface with dignity while she made toast and coffee and boiled eggs, bearing them triumphantly back to bed. So for most of our early married life we indulged in the luxury of breakfast in bed, succeeding by this method in starting the day more or less together.

Sue was a born homemaker. While I went off to work, she threw herself with energy and enthusiasm into cleaning and curtain-making, garden clearing and exploring the local shops for bargains. I came home each evening to delicious cooking smells and one of her mother's well-tried recipes or one that Susie had made up herself with imaginative flair. We tackled the major painting and decorating jobs together and had enormous fun. It never occurred to either of us that we might disagree on anything. If it had, I'm sure we'd have been horrified and dismissed the idea as quite impossible.

So our first argument was a major upset, breaking rudely and unexpectedly into our happiness. It blew up from nowhere like a summer storm.

We'd got as far as the bathroom. It was in a sorry state, with peeling and cracked paint stretching round the walls above white tiles which we didn't like. The tiles were quite serviceable and not in too bad a condition so we'd decided to keep them. At about waist level a thin line of black tiles cut the room in half, but again we had decided to put up with the striped effect. The problem arose over the colour we should paint the walls. I hadn't given it much thought, but Susie seemed to have raced ahead of me.

'Blue would be ideal,' she pronounced, as we stood surveying the scene after supper that fateful evening. 'You remember the blue spare room at home? A shade like that would give a lovely sea freshness in here, wouldn't it? I've always loved that colour. We could do the ceiling the same.'

As it happened, I had never liked blue very much and the idea of a blue bathroom didn't appeal at all. But I was even more bothered by the fact that Sue hadn't consulted me and yet already seemed quite decided.

My silence became tangible, and Sue must have read the disapproval on my face.

'Come on, Max,' she ventured a little uncertainly. 'Whatever is wrong with blue?'

'I think it's rather cold and uninviting,' I said.

'But, Max,' Sue was indignant. 'You used to stay in the blue spare room at home quite happily. Didn't you think it was nice?'

I hadn't liked it much, but somehow I couldn't say that just then. Instinctively, I knew Sue would be hurt.

'I just don't think it would be a good colour for the bathroom,' I said lamely.

I couldn't meet her eye. It occurred to me rather irrationally that Sue was trying to recreate the home where she'd grown up and the thought made me unaccountably angry. I suddenly remembered something. After our first weekend visit to her parents as a married couple, Sue had cried on the way home. I'd been talking eagerly about our next project on the house when I'd noticed the tears running down her cheeks. Alarmed, I'd asked what was wrong but she'd said it was nothing really. She just felt sad all of a sudden. At the time I'd thought it was probably quite a natural reaction to leaving a home she'd loved very much and a close family. I'd made a few sympathetic noises and then forgotten the whole incident. Now it rushed back to my mind with ominous significance.

Sue was wringing her hands unhappily, but her mouth was still set in a determined line. I knew that if I tried to say anything more I'd be shouting at her and that would be unbearable. We'd never shouted at each other. We'd never been in conflict before and the whole thing was so unexpected and unwelcome that neither of us knew what to do.

I had never subscribed to the theory that a good row clears the air. It always seemed to me that the hurt caused by such an exchange could far outweigh the so-called benefits and not be at all easy to heal once the dust had settled. Sue was simply not the argumentative type, more often laughing than cross. So we stood wrestling with our feelings in stubborn and confused silence until I suggested in measured tones that we went for a walk. Without looking at each other, we went downstairs, pulled on our coats, locked the door behind us and marched out into the cool evening.

It had rained and the air was damp. Our breath froze in little clouds around us and I filled my lungs deeply. I couldn't believe that we had fallen out over something so trivial. And I was even more furious that I didn't know how to handle the situation. Sue stomped along at my side and minutes went by before we hesitantly began to talk about what was happening. Bit by bit, and in slow, controlled sentences, it all came out.

'I didn't mean it to seem as if I'd already made up my mind about the colour.' Sue was perplexed at my attempts to explain why I was cross. 'I think – I think I expected you to like it because we like so many of the same things.'

I managed to convey that where the colour blue was concerned, she was wrong in her assumption. 'And anyway, I don't see why we should have it just because it was at your place.'

There, it was out. Perhaps I should have put it more gently. Perhaps I was wrong ...

'I don't think I wanted blue just because it was at home,' Sue said. She wasn't defensive, she was thoughtful. 'But perhaps that came into it and I didn't realise. We all thought it was a fantastic colour, so I just didn't question it for the bathroom.'

I took her hand. 'Well, perhaps the fact that we *didn't* like it much at the farm coloured my thinking, too,' I said wryly.

The anger was draining away. We weren't putting across coldly our points of view any more, we were trying to understand.

'But honestly, Max, I'd much rather find a colour we both like. I really wouldn't want to paint it anything you didn't want.'

When we got back to the house we went straight to the bathroom and agreed that peach walls would look very nice, but I don't think either of us really liked it when it was all done. We may have resolved the situation as well as we knew how at the time, but the deeper issues were still to be fully understood and tackled. We'd been rudely awakened to the fact that 'happy ever after' was an ideal, not an instant reality, and that there were differences between us that weren't always going to fit together comfortably. That was enough to take for the time being.

Later, we would learn to laugh at the 'baggage' we brought with us into our marriage – preferences and prejudices that were rooted in our family backgrounds. And only as we got to know each other better were we able to accept the different ways we looked on things and did things instead of feeling threatened by them. At first, as we tried to understand what went wrong over the bathroom, it seemed horrifying that we'd argued. It seemed a failure. Whereas what we had to learn was that conflict was inevitable at some time or another between two people who lived together – yes, and who loved each other. We were only human after all, and though that couldn't be an excuse, it was none the less a fact of our very ordinary situation. Hoping arguments wouldn't happen or running from them when they did would never be a solution, but it took much more than the bathroom incident for us to realise this and to learn how to cope with disagreement.

When we moved house again many years later, Sue had a million ideas for decoration before we'd even unpacked the suitcases – some things never change! But I knew by then that she was made like that and, in the same way, she knew that I needed a bit more time to consider things before getting stuck in. We were both prepared to give way to each other, and to say what we thought without getting heated. And we'd long since agreed that we wouldn't argue unless it was really worth an argument. I can't help wondering, though, what colour we'd paint the bathroom at Rowan Cottage if we had to decide on it today.

In those early days of marriage, it wasn't just Sue I had to get used to living with – but myself! There were sides of my nature that I hardly knew existed and that mysteriously made an appearance once someone else was around. And I didn't always like what came to the surface.

The garden was a focus for some of this new self-awareness. We'd started the job of clearing and weeding almost as soon as we'd arrived, and had unearthed a rockery and even a small sunken garden. To our delight there were also one or two fruit trees laden with juicy apples and pears, which we often picked and ate while we were digging.

We both worked very happily in the garden as a rule, and relished making plans together for its development. But whereas I knew lots about how to rebuild the sunken garden and could knock up a timber structure down the main path so roses could be coaxed to grow over it, I was hopeless at the business of choosing plants and deciding where they'd look best. Susie was the expert here, but instead of welcoming her superior knowledge on the subject, I found myself feeling uncomfortably resentful. Poor Susie could never be sure what reaction she'd get to a suggestion about this or that plant. As often as not I'd be enthusiastic, preferring to keep my hard feelings to myself since there was absolutely no justification for them whatsoever. Sometimes, though, if I was feeling particularly sensitive, I would appear diffident, or agree guardedly as if I might have a better idea, but of course I never did. At worst, I would keep a stubborn silence in a corner and feign indifference to the positioning of a plant or shrub.

Sue must have noticed that I didn't always enter into the creation of the garden with exuberance, but if she said nothing it was because I gave her no reason to think anything was wrong. How could she have known what was going on in my head if I didn't tell her? And yet when I was banging in a nail particularly hard, or probing feverishly at a stubborn weed, I minded that she didn't appear to notice that I wasn't one hundred per cent happy. I smouldered at that as much as I did because she was better at something than I was. It was a ridiculous situation, and it was made worse because I knew how silly I was being. But of course this made it all the more difficult to admit anything to Sue. My pride was hurt in the first place, and I'd have to swallow what was left in confessing my childish resentment.

We talked about it much later.

'You felt threatened?' Susie prompted gently on that occasion.

'Well, I thought I wasn't being a proper husband.'

Sue giggled despite herself. 'Sorry, Max, I'm listening really. But how could you have thought that just because ...'

I cut her short. 'I mean I felt I should know best in every situation, and if I didn't I was failing you somehow. It was the role I felt I should live up to as your husband.' How much pressure we put on ourselves sometimes by trying to assume a role instead of working out for ourselves and with our partner what each has to bring to the relationship. And how much heartache can be avoided if we're honest with each other from the start about our expectations and personal needs. As far as Sue's capability in the garden was concerned, however, I knew there was a good dose of pride in my reaction.

'I had to learn that I wasn't the superman I was trying to crack myself up to be,' I confessed with a rueful grin.

Sue hooted with laughter and I joined in heartily, able to laugh at myself then.

'It didn't make it any easier,' I went on, still laughing, 'when you *sang* as you planted.' Sue threw her head back in helpless delight. 'You ... you were having such fun,' I gasped, 'and I was so miserable.'

It would clearly have been easier for both of us if I had been able to verbalise how I was feeling over the garden sooner than I managed, but talking about my feelings has never been something that has come naturally to me. They say this is a particularly male characteristic, and certainly Sue found it hard to get used to. Of course she'd known before we were married that I wasn't as open as she was about things, but confessed later that she hadn't appreciated just how significant a difference this was between us. In any situation where I felt unsure or defensive for some reason, my reaction was to withdraw rather than talk it out. Needless to say, it didn't help communication.

I did improve as trust built up between us and as I recognised this tendency in myself. It was a learning process, and didn't happen overnight. It's easy to be impatient in the early years of marriage, wanting everything to be sorted out quickly and worrying if it's not. But there's no substitute for time that is used to get to know each other even better, and to learn from experience. In fact, there are probably few things more exciting than a whole lifetime in which to hone and deepen and enjoy a relationship.

As the days rolled by, Sue and I came to agree on who did what in running our home. There were some definite areas of responsibility that were mine, such as structural maintenance on the house – and particularly in all matters of electricity.

'Are you sure that's all right, Max?' Sue would ask nervously if I fixed an electric plug or rigged up a new appliance.

'Perfectly.' And usually it was. But not always.

'You know that light switch you checked yesterday,' Sue remarked one day soon after I had come in from work. I cast my mind back to the evening before when I'd flicked the living-room light switch on and off and checked the wiring because Sue had seen sparks coming from it.

'It seemed okay,' I recalled. 'No sparks once I'd poked around a bit.'

'I'm sure I saw some today. Could you have another look?' I did so, but found nothing wrong at all. Sue seemed reassured when I told her, but over the next couple of weeks she found a dozen different faults with the wiring system that she relayed to me with an ever-increasing anxiety.

'Perhaps we should get someone professional in to look at it,' she suggested at last. At once my feathers were decidedly ruffled. Didn't she trust me to keep things in good order? 'We might even ask for an estimate for rewiring the place,' she went on. 'It's very antiquated, isn't it?' I didn't answer, but made a disapproving face. I had made allowances for Sue's nervousness about electricity, but this was getting ridiculous.

'I'll think about it,' was all I said.

Shortly afterwards, a colleague at work happened to mention that he'd just had his house rewired and it had cost him ninety pounds. I gulped as he mentioned the sum. That was way beyond anything we could afford. It represented nearly two months' salary or a sizeable hole in our building society account. That decided me once and for all.

'We simply can't afford it,' I said categorically to Sue.

She was not impressed. 'One of us is going to get killed, that's all,' she countered. 'Either that or the whole place will burn down.'

Then to my astonishment she burst into tears.

'You don't seem to be taking this seriously,' she sobbed.

'Of course I am.' And then, as the sobbing increased, 'We're not made of money, you know.' That didn't help either, and I could think of nothing else to say. A minute passed and Sue wiped her face fiercely and sniffed, looking abashed at her outburst but unrepentant.

I felt an urgent desire to escape this painful deadlock and think things through. Abruptly, I headed for the study with a mumbled excuse about having to sort out my papers for the next day, and was gone from the room before Sue had time to respond. Safely next door, I heard her clattering the plates and running the tap to wash up. When I was sure she wouldn't follow me, I turned up the building society statement. There was just enough money there to go ahead with the rewiring. The decision was suddenly clear.

Sue was bent over the sink when I came back into the kitchen.

'Would you like a cup of coffee?' I asked.

'Thanks,' was her quiet reply.

I went over to her with the kettle and began to fill it from the tap.

'Sue.' She didn't raise her head. 'I've looked at the building society statement and we can afford to have the house rewired. You're right, and I'm sorry if ...' The kettle was nearly knocked to the floor as I was caught in a wet, soapy embrace.

'Thank you so much,' said Sue. 'I didn't mean to be difficult, but I really was worried.'

As I held her closely, the ninety pounds seemed a small price to pay for Sue's peace of mind and our harmony. There were better investments to make than merely financial ones. My wife's happiness for one thing.

'I'm sorry,' I repeated, 'I should have appreciated how you were feeling.'

She squeezed me tighter in response.

'What a relief,' she said with her old brightness when we eventually disentangled ourselves. 'It feels like we're in love again.'

That night, I lay awake long after Sue had drifted off to sleep. Everywhere was very quiet. The streetlight outside cast shadows across the room, picking out a corner of the wardrobe that had generously been donated by my parents, along with the bed and chest of drawers. Most of our furniture had been given to us in fact, or found in the junk shops we loved to frequent in search of bargains. How lucky we were, how blessed to have such kind families and now a home of our own. How easy it could be to spoil everything, to sour the loving relationship we longed to preserve.

'Lord,' I prayed silently, 'we do need your help.'

A gust of wind came through the open window and the

curtain billowed slightly. My thoughts ran on. Didn't it say in Ephesians that wives should submit to their husbands? 'Was I wrong then, Lord, to expect Susie to acquiesce to my decision?' From somewhere far away, a dog barked. The sound carried through the quiet night, and then stopped. 'I don't mean she has to do what I say all the time of course,' I defended myself. 'But if we disagree, someone has to make a decision, and I thought it should be mine. We've talked about it. Susie thinks it's biblical, too.' Then the words of the second part of the passage in Ephesians emblazoned themselves across my thoughts. 'And husbands, love your wives.' Open-eyed, I stared at the ceiling. 'I do love Susie, Lord.' Her words that evening came back to me with sudden new meaning – we're in love again. She hadn't felt I was loving her then. I don't suppose I was. 'Husbands, love your wives.' The Bible asks wives to submit to the loving direction of their husbands, not to their selfish desires. There were two distinct guidelines, and they had to work hand in hand or they wouldn't work at all.

I closed my eyes, and slept.

On Mondays, my work seemed a particularly un-welcome interruption to our togetherness. We often went for long walks in the country at the weekends, stomping out in all weathers and taking a picnic if it wasn't too bleak. The thought of donning my pin-stripes and joining the commuters into the City never had much appeal when my lungs were full of fresh air.

Catching the train in the morning was invariably a scramble, since the serious business of actually leaving the house was left until the last minute. Susie would walk briskly at my side to the station or sometimes drop me off by car if we were very late. The ticket-barrier where we exchanged a fond, but usually hasty, kiss was like the dividing line between two very distinct worlds. Sue would stand the other side of it and watch the train pull away from the station, while I found a seat and settled myself among the suits and brief-cases and open morning papers.

I could almost feel the expression on my face becoming as fixed and uncommunicative as those around me. When Susie disappeared from view, the warm and secure world of home was shut out of sight for the rest of the day.

I enjoyed my work, however, and once inside the office and racing to meet deadlines or complete a particularly complicated audit, I stopped wishing I could be at home with Susie, or striding through the countryside. Being an articled clerk was nothing if not a challenge, and as part of the large City firm of Peat, Marwick, Mitchell and Co., I was at the centre of intense and stimulating activity.

But at the end of the day, the transition to the other side of the barrier was no easier than in the mornings.

Sometimes I would get home from work full to bursting point of all that had happened during the day, and pour it out in graphic detail to a patient Sue. She could identify with some of what I told her because she could identify closely with me, but other intricacies of office life left her baffled. It wasn't really surprising since she had no experience of the business environment, but even while I recognised this and tried to explain it carefully I would sometimes feel hurt if she didn't enter into it all in the spirit I would have liked.

I remember telling her once in great detail about a particular crisis and how we'd sorted everything out in the nick of time. Admittedly it had meant staying in the office until midnight for a couple of days, but I was stung by her response.

'What a fuss!' she said with disdain.

'A fuss? Sue, if we hadn't met that deadline we might have lost one of our most important clients.'

'I know, but all that frantic rushing around and those late nights just for a bit of money!'

I gave up trying to explain it to her. She busied herself with the meal and by the time we'd eaten, my exasperation at her apparent dismissal of an important achievement had melted away. But the tension remained.

Some days the barrier between my two worlds was less apparent. I would hold the picture of Sue at home in the forefront of my mind and be at one remove from all the activity of the office, even though I was completing what was on my desk. I felt linked to our little house in Orpington by some invisible thread, and on those days it was easier to adjust when I came home in the evenings.

There was the temptation too, when I had thrown myself into the day and all its challenges, to keep it to myself when I got home. This wasn't a conscious decision, but I realised it was happening one day when Sue asked me about a particular job I'd been involved in.

'I meant to ask you about it yesterday,' she continued rather apologetically. 'I think I got side-tracked with all I wanted to tell you myself.'

In fact, I had completed the job a few days previously, but must have failed to mention it.

Before I could say anything, Sue launched into several questions in an effort to make up for what she saw as partly her fault. I was soon reliving it all for her, and realised how much I had actually missed sharing it with her.

I don't think I appreciated then how easily we could have cut ourselves off from each other if I had gone on keeping my work to myself, or only sharing it in superficial detail. Patience and understanding were required from both of us, and obviously we didn't always manage to have a sufficient amount of either. It was particularly hard for me, for instance, when Sue's reaction to what I was telling her was critical. Sometimes her lack of trust in the business world was something I just had to treat with patience, but at other times she was my conscience – prompting me back to God's standards when the world was proving beguiling. A frown would wrinkle her forehead and warn me of what was to come, and I would jump behind my defence line ready to justify whatever practice she was concerned about.

45

'Really, Max, it can't be right to spend so much time chatting away about fishing when you're supposed to be working.'

'I *don't* chat about fishing. I hardly know anything about it.'

'But you were just telling me how interesting it sounded from what your two colleagues were saying.'

'Well, if they have a mutual passion for fishing, why shouldn't they talk about it?'

'They're getting paid huge salaries to keep their heads down.'

I laughed at Sue's emphasis on the 'huge', despite myself. Her instinct for fairness couldn't accept that I, as an articled clerk who had to occupy himself with much the same sort of work as his superiors, although obviously at a different level, should get such a meagre salary by comparison.

'But you can't keep your head down all the time,' I told her. 'If we didn't have some light relief we really would collapse with the heart attacks you keep warning me about.'

She conceded that one. But other things worried her much more, such as the apparent all-consuming passion in the City to earn as much money as possible, and the sooner the better. Her objection was the more disconcerting because I found the materialistic bias of the office difficult to live with too. Some days my head rang with advice about buying certain shares and selling others, trading in such and such a car for one that was better, investing in a house in a certain area because it would increase in value, and so on and so on. There must be something badly wrong if every other concern and value was subordinated to the drive for financial gain.

But I couldn't help admiring the senior partner's Rolls. And I could understand the appeal of a comfortable house in a nice area, a luxurious life style and holidays in the sun. There was a seductive attraction about the materialistic world I entered daily, and I was no less immune to its

46

charms than anyone else.

As an articled clerk, I wasn't under the sort of pressure my senior colleagues had to contend with. I rarely needed to work long hours, and since my salary could hardly justify my doing so anyway no one expected me to stay late in the office every day. Some of the senior partners worked ridiculous hours, however, and although I knew they were often motivated by genuine enjoyment and excitement, I could see the price they had to pay written all over their haggard faces. Was it really worth what must be a serious threat to their health? And what about their family life?

I didn't stop long at that stage to think about the future, or to wonder how I should cope when the pressure hotted up. If God meant me to stay in the business world, His help and guidance would be near at hand. I knew that I would need Him to keep me from being seduced by the atmosphere of driving ambition and competitiveness, and any thoughts that fat salary cheques were an aim in themselves. 'The love of money is a root of all kinds of evil,' Paul wrote in his first letter to Timothy (6: 10) 'and those who desire to be rich bring all kinds of sorrow upon themselves'.

Later, I was to realise that my particular sensitivity to the difficulties of being a Christian in the business world was the beginning of an indication that God might be leading me elsewhere. For the time being, however, there were no obvious pointers in a different direction so I tried to apply myself diligently to my studies and to my work. The course I was doing in preparation for my final exams took up the train journeys to and from the office. I didn't want it to eat into precious time with Susie, so kept the papers locked in my brief-case while I was at home.

It wasn't long before something new was taking up our time. In fact, we got stuck into it very quickly – against all the advice of our Christian friends.

3

'Look for the right church before you buy a house,' we'd been told by several people before we were married. Once the church had been decided, a house could be found in the same area.

It was good advice, meant to encourage us to make God's priorities our own from the very start of our marriage and to ensure that we got involved in a lively, supportive fellowship where we could grow as Christians. But we weren't able to do things in quite this order, although we were committed to seeking God's guidance for our home and fellowship. We did the next best thing, and made sure there were several lively churches in the area before Dad got on with his purchase.

We lost no time in finding out which church we should go to once we'd moved. On our very first Saturday evening, we sat at our enamel-topped kitchen table, cups of coffee in hand as was so often our practice, and discussed where we should go the following morning. Sue made a list of the nearby churches and we scanned it eagerly.

'Not this one.' I crossed the first name out. 'I gather the vicar preaches from the newspapers most of the time, and believes they're more up to date than the Bible.'

Neither of us wanted to go to a church where the Bible was not upheld fully and unreservedly as God's Word. We could never commit ourselves to a fellowship based on something different.

We knew we needed good teaching, too. There was a big difference between sermons which put across interesting ideas for discussion and those which offered real spiritual nourishment and guidance for practical Christian living.

'I think we can cross this one off, too,' Sue said, pointing to the second name on the list. 'Their big emphasis is on social issues.'

I hesitated. It was important for any church to be active in a practical way in the community, but not at the expense of Christ's challenge to 'make disciples' which was part and parcel of His ministry to the poor and underprivileged. A church which didn't have a concern for evangelism could hardly be the place for us. Sue was right, and I crossed off the second name.

Next on the list was a Baptist church.

'How about that one?' Sue asked. 'It's just down the road.'

I raised my eyebrows in mock surprise.

'But you've never been a Baptist in your life.'

'Good time to start,' she laughed.

Sue's faith had been nurtured in the Anglican tradition, and since I had been brought up among Open Brethren I didn't have much connection with the Baptists either. But I had been baptised by full immersion when I was at university, wanting to make a public confession of my faith now that I was old enough to make my own decision. I'd been baptised as a child of 12 at my father's suggestion and quietly at home in what was known as a household service. I was sprinkled with water which wasn't quite the same as the full ducking in the baptistry, and I felt the latter was closer to the biblical practice somehow, since after all John the Baptist made use of a whole river when he baptised people.

'We'll take a bath towel along for you just in case,' I teased. 'They might want to pop you in the baptistry before you attend the service.'

We knew God's family extended across all denominations so neither of us felt committed to one rather than another. The important thing was the quality of life in the church. There was an Anglican church on our list which we'd heard was very lively, so we decided to try it in the evening, and the Baptist church was earmarked for the morning.

We enjoyed the first service very much and probably could have thrown in our lot with the Baptists very comfortably. Neither of us felt so convinced about it as to forget the Anglican service in the evening, however, and agreed we should still go along. We were intrigued to see how different it might be and prayed that God would highlight which church was right for us.

Before we even sat down at Christchurch, at least six people squeezed my hand in welcome. The sermon was full of solid Bible teaching and the whole service was reverent yet full of life and variety. When it was over, we were greeted by several more people, including the vicar, and were even invited to the homes of two friendly couples. Such warmth and kindness were overwhelming. It was another of our priorities to find a church where we could feel really at home and part of a fellowship in which people cared about one another and didn't just rush in and out of the services without stopping to talk.

As yet another person waylaid us at the church door, I felt sure this was where we were meant to be. Every item on my mental checklist had been ticked. I was eager to hear Susie's reaction.

'I'd like to go to Christchurch again,' was her comment over the hot chocolate later after we'd weighed up the experiences of the day.

As if to confirm our decision, we had a visitor just a few days afterwards.

'Hello,' smiled Canon Herbert Taylor from the doorstep. 'We met last Sunday. I hope I'm not interrupting you.'

Another cup of coffee was quickly made and Canon Taylor didn't seem to mind in the least sitting at our kitchen table to drink it. He told us all about the church and its many activities and asked us about ourselves. We responded gladly to his genuine interest, but when he heard about the difficulties we'd had in obtaining the house he frowned.

'I'm sorry to hear that. Oh I'm very sorry to hear that.' He shook his head. 'Do you mind if I make a suggestion? With your consent I'd like to pray for this house. It's been an unhappy place, full of the heartbreak of that poor woman and her husband. I believe we should pray specifically that God will reinhabit it and bless your life here.'

We agreed readily. I couldn't think of anything more appropriate when we'd barely been in our new home a week than for it to be rededicated to the Lord through the kindness and concern of this godly man.

Having already given us a generous portion of his time, he then went into every single room and prayed in each one. We bowed our heads with him. 'Lord, you know in this kitchen there must have been many arguments, and perhaps few people welcomed. May that all be buried in the past, and may this room become one of hospitality and gladness.' 'Lord, bring joy to this bedroom. May it be a place of shared happiness and not conflict.' For each room, he had an appropriate word, and by the time we returned to the kitchen the house seemed aglow with new promise.

The canon reached for his coat. 'Well, I'm glad to have got to know you a little better.'

I grasped his outstretched hand. 'Thank you so much for what you've done. We'll always be grateful.' He nodded and turned to leave. 'Oh and we'll see you next Sunday,' I added.

'Delighted to hear it,' came the enthusiastic reply. 'I hope you'll be happy with us.'

We settled in quickly and soon began to wonder if there was anything specific we could contribute to the church. This is where we went against another piece of advice we'd been given before we were married. It seemed it wasn't a good idea to get too involved in church activities in the first year of marriage. Time was needed for each other and for building the foundation of our marriage from which we could eventually serve the Christian community.

We respected the wisdom in this advice, too, but a year seemed a very long time to us.

'It may be the right thing for some people to do,' Sue had said when we first talked it over, 'but I'm sure I'll want to get going straightaway.'

I felt the same. We'd known each other a long time before we were married so it wasn't as if we needed lots of time together in the way some couples might, and although there was a long way to go in growing really close, we felt the foundation of our marriage was as firm as it need be for making an active contribution to the church. Apart from that, neither of us was the kind of person to be part of a church and *not* be fully involved. The one didn't exist without the other. We'd always got stuck in and had loved it, so it seemed quite natural to do so now.

At Christchurch, we didn't have long to wait.

'I know you're still quite new,' the curate began apologetically after the morning service on a crisp, autumn Sunday, 'but we wondered whether you might consider helping us with the youth work.'

He, Christopher Barnes, looked searchingly at our faces and I caught Sue's eye. She grinned and my own broad smile seemed to baffle the young man who'd posed his question so carefully.

'We'd been praying about what we might do to help,' I explained. He nodded at once, understanding.

'And we've actually worked with young people before,' Sue broke in.

He nodded again, an eagerness now lighting his eyes. I knew how he felt. It was one of those moments which God seemed to have initiated in a very specific way. Although we knew little about the young people's group that met every Sunday evening, I felt an excitement deep in the pit of my stomach.

'Tell us more about it and we'll be delighted to think it over,' I urged Christopher.

He lost no time in inviting us along that evening so we duly turned up at the vicarage after the 6.30 service. Our welcome was hardly less warm than on the first Sunday we'd come to the church.

'Hello, so glad you could come.'

'Christopher's trying to rope you into this, is he?'

'Didn't I hear that you play the guitar, Max?'

We'd already met a number of the young people who greeted us so cheerily, and were soon joining in the animated chatter, clutching steaming cups of coffee. By the time Christopher arrived, any formal introduction to the others was unnecessary. We all settled down in various chairs and empty spaces on the floor – even the fair-sized vicarage sitting-room was hard pressed to accommodate about twenty people. Someone got out a guitar and a time of worship was quickly underway, followed by a Bible study led by Christopher and much lively discussion that could have gone on far into the night.

'I could see you enjoyed yourselves,' Christopher commented afterwards, and we had to admit it had been a great evening. The curate didn't push us to make any decision about future involvement there and then, but we quickly agreed together that we would love to help him lead the group. Memories of our beach missions flooded back as we acknowledged how much we enjoyed being with young people. The Lord was very gracious to give us such an opportunity to use our experience of leading worship and Bible study, particularly when we both found it so satisfying and so much fun. And we were glad we would be doing it together. It would be our first joint effort as a married couple in the Lord's service.

The following Sunday I took along my guitar and it wasn't long before we settled happily into the weekly routine. Since there were often activities on a Saturday too, our weekends became very full and busy.

But Christopher had another idea up his sleeve.

'A coffee bar,' he told us excitedly. 'Think of all those youngsters on the estate out there who would never dream of darkening the doors of a church. They would feel at home in a coffee bar, if we got the right atmosphere. You know, music perhaps and the lights not too bright. How ever are we going to reach them with the gospel otherwise?'

He had a point of course. The young people who came to our Sunday evening group were mostly from secure homes and had been church-goers much of their lives. They had an awareness of God and an understanding of what it meant to follow Christ, and many had made personal commitments, but there was no obvious way into such a group for youngsters without the church background. The opportunities for them to hear and respond to the love of Christ were practically non-existent and we had a responsibility to them. Christopher's enthusiasm was catching.

Somehow, he managed to persuade a wary Parish Church Council to back the coffee-bar project and plans got underway to convert the church basement. Willing hands cleaned and painted, barrels were found to serve as tables and chairs and I helped to build a counter for refreshments. In a few months we were ready to invite our first guests, and our prayers and preparation were rewarded by a large number of young people crowding in, curious to find out what this new Saturday night's entertainment was all about.

It was one thing to be zealous to communicate the gospel to those who might never have heard it before, but it was quite another to do it. None of us had much experience of tough, aggressive teenagers, and it was hard to find any point of contact let alone introduce God into the conversation.

'Did you enjoy tonight's talk then?' I eventually plucked up courage to ask a bunch of leather-jacketed boys, in what I hoped was a casual way. Chris had stood up halfway through the evening and given some warm words of welcome alongside some challenging ones from the Bible. I thought he put things very clearly and helpfully, but the boys didn't seem of the same opinion. A couple of them giggled, perhaps embarrassed or perhaps just dismissive of such a daft question. They looked bored, and after some more shuffling of feet, one of them said it was all right, wasn't it? He said it in such a way as to defy any further comment. I'd know better than to employ such a direct approach next time.

Motor-bikes were the answer. They all seemed to have them, and since I genuinely didn't know much about the different makes and their various virtues, my questions about them were quite genuine. That broke the ice, and after a few weeks I felt that at last some rapport was being established.

It was uphill work. The normal pattern of the evening was informal, with just a short talk given by Christopher or myself about a God who was real and His relevance to daily living. We didn't push an evangelistic message too strongly to start with, feeling that it might simply be too much for kids who apparently hadn't thought much about God at all. We didn't want to alienate them or lose their initial interest. We also asked one or two of the young people from the youth group to stand up and give their testimonies very briefly, saying what Christianity was all about for them and what difference God made in their lives. Otherwise most of our energies were spent in trying to engage our guests in conversation. Some of the young Christians entered heart and soul into the endeavour alongside the leaders, although we all struggled one way or another in this new situation.

It was Saturday afternoon about four weeks after we'd opened the coffee bar when Sue and I heard the front-door bell. We were trying to catch up on some of the weeding in the garden.

'I'll go,' and Sue bounded inside. I couldn't believe it when she ushered three lads from the coffee bar into the garden. Sue looked quite comic standing beside them, her hands grubby from gardening and an expression of utter bewilderment on her face.

'Goin' tonight?' one of them asked.

'Oh – yes, definitely,' I said, busily brushing mud from my trousers.

'Thought we'd drop in as we were passin'. Didn't think you'd mind.'

'No, no – not at all.' It was amazing they'd felt free to call by.

The kettle was on in no time, and our kitchen became the centre of a heated discussion about the pros and cons of putting your own bike together. Sue and I exchanged delighted glances. The lads had relaxed very quickly, and they opened up a lot more easily than in the coffee bar. We felt significantly nearer to establishing a real friendship.

After that, Alan, Paul and George quite often came to call on us. They took us as they found us and seemed happy just to chat and drink coffee, and sometimes they brought fish and chips to munch. They too seemed to value the bond created by this new contact with us, and their attitude in the coffee bar subtly changed as a result. They assumed a role of protection. They ticked off rudeness and threatened recrimination for inconsiderate noise, and while at first we were grateful for this support it also had effects which tested our resources even more.

On one particular evening, Paul clearly got fed up with all the noise and chatter that was going on while Christopher tried to give his talk. It was very hard to hold the youngsters' attention at the best of times, and very often our new-found friends' efforts to shut everyone up only served to add to the noise. On this occasion, Paul decided more drastic action was needed. Spying out the source of most of the problem, Paul – who was as broad as he was tall – leaned over and grabbed the offending youngster by the scruff of the neck. Hoisting him vertically into the air, he bawled his objection into the lad's ear and then dropped him unceremoniously back into his chair. His action was most effective. The hall was stunned into silence.

'Sorry about that, sir,' Paul said deferentially to

Christopher, who cleared his throat hurriedly and tried to pick up the thread of what he'd been saying.

Not surprisingly, the lad who'd been subjected to Paul's corrective treatment wasn't at all pleased and I watched his stony face with foreboding. Sure enough, he was out for trouble, and that night I had my first encounter with a knuckleduster – not literally, since I managed to duck in time, but it was only because we'd learnt to recognise the signs that we managed to prevent a full-scale fight. We were shaken, and thankful that the incident had gone no further. But it was only a beginning.

I'd expected the coffee-bar ministry to become easier once we'd got used to it and established contact with the kids, but instead we seemed to be coming up against even more problems. I'd hoped that my own nervousness would lessen, too. I hadn't admitted it to anyone, but I was pretty scared inside. Sometimes I worried about Sue when she was chatting on the other side of the coffee bar, too far away for me to protect her if trouble broke out. What on earth had we let ourselves in for? I might not have minded so much if I felt we were making any headway, but there was little evidence that the Gospel message was getting through.

When I wasn't feeling harassed or confused by the gangs who came to the coffee bar, my heart went out to them. Many came from broken homes and had never known the security of a loving family. Others had been in trouble with the law and seemed unable to break out of a treadmill of petty crime. I longed for them to find the real freedom of a new life in Christ and to know that they were loved by God.

'How can we take them further?' I lamented to Sue. 'Their interest only goes so far. How can we help them to go away from the coffee bar with something lasting, something that will make a difference to them?'

Christopher was no less concerned than we were, and for a time we made a much more concerted effort to come alongside the young people individually and to build up friendships. We tried asking one or two to the Sunday youth fellowship, but although our invitations weren't rebuffed they weren't taken up either.

'I'll see what Robert is doing,' was a stock reply, or David or Alan. They would all seek safety in numbers and make that an excuse not to commit themselves. In the end no one came along.

'Perhaps we should make the talks more evangelistic,' suggested Christopher. It seemed a good idea. The kids surely understood enough now to respond to a more direct challenge.

So we tried it, but it coincided with a surge of new people from the estate that split our audience in two. The aggression between the older supporters of the coffee bar and the newcomers escalated into a sort of gang warfare, and the incident with the knuckleduster now seemed like an ominous warning. There were fights outside the church, bottles thrown and windows broken. Understandably some of the congregation began to question what we were doing and we had to defend ourselves to them as well as cope with a situation that seemed increasingly out of our control. We redoubled our prayers for protection and a real breakthrough.

One Saturday, it all came to a head. Someone had taken our side once too often and there were muttered threats to deal with the 'vicar's little yes man'. It was almost time for the coffee bar to close and I watched with growing alarm as a group gathered force and the lads whispered and nudged each other. Suddenly I knew there was no time to waste and, locating Sue gathering coffee cups, I thrust the car keys into her hand.

'Listen,' I whispered fiercely. 'Do exactly as I say. Go and unlock the car and stand by the back door ready to open it when I come.'

Sue looked at me in surprise, taken aback by my commanding tone.

'Did you hear what I said?' She had to understand. 'I think there's going to be some trouble – hurry.'

She hesitated a moment longer, then slipped quickly outside.

The helpers from the youth group were starting to tidy up, and the coffee bar was emptying. The gang had disappeared but a glance into the church carpark revealed them clustered together, waiting. To my horror, I saw the flash of a knife.

I raced back inside and frantically searched for the 'vicar's yes man', urging one or two more of the leaders to join me. To my great relief, the youngster was still there.

'We're going to take you home.' I made him put on my anorak, hoping this would disguise him a little. Startled, he obeyed my urgent command to follow me out to the car and, with the others protectively at our side, we walked determinedly past his aggressors. I didn't look back. Susie was by the car, tense and grim-faced, and we bundled the boy into the back seat and safety.

'We're getting absolutely nowhere,' I exploded once we got home. I was still shaking. 'We're just providing a cosy venue for warfare.'

Sue put her arm round me, but the floodgates of my frustration and disappointment were well and truly open. 'We've achieved nothing at that coffee bar. Not one of those lads has made a commitment after all these months. We're just bashing our heads against a brick wall.'

I felt like giving up. What was the point of carrying on? We might as well close the coffee bar and be done with it. But I didn't say that. I stopped short of voicing out loud to Sue my total discouragement and sense of failure. I was supposed to be her protector and provider, the strong partner in our marriage. What would she think if she knew how very small and helpless I felt just then?

'What have we done wrong?' I threw out despairingly.

'Perhaps we're just trying to force God's timing,' came the reply after a pause. 'There has to be sowing before there's reaping after all. It's bound to take time.'

Her wisdom was lost on me, and the fact that she was probably right only irritated me even more.

'Time?' I was incredulous. 'But we've already taken time.'

'We're probably more impatient than God.'

I was silent. We were in too deep – out of our depth in fact. Did God really want us to carry on? And I suddenly wondered if He had called us to this or if we had jumped in with nothing but human enthusiasm.

'I know you're feeling rotten,' Sue said gently. There was no recrimination in her voice. Someone else might have told me to buck up, or said it wasn't like me to be discouraged, but Sue seemed to accept me, even though I wasn't being the person I wanted to be just then. I realised she knew me very well in fact, and probably was aware of my coward's heart. I was surprised that she wasn't turning away with an excuse about making coffee or something.

'I love you Susie.'

A big hug and a kiss, and I thought rather ruefully that God couldn't have provided me with a better helpmate for the work in the coffee bar. I could see that Sue was already trying to think of some practical solution, and I marvelled again at how steady and level-headed she was. It took a lot to get her ruffled.

'What about laying on something separate for the new youngsters,' she suggested, right on cue.

'I suppose you're going to want to build another coffee bar,' I retorted ungraciously.

'No – I was thinking we could take some of them away for the weekend. We know a few of them well enough, don't we?'

Out of the frying pan and into the fire – and it was rather like that. A bold idea, indeed. We must have been full of naive enthusiasm to take it on, but we did and had a predictably hard time. We should have guessed there wouldn't be much interest in nature walks or bird sanctuaries from a bunch of tough youngsters.

So we muddled on. Prayerfully, we grew more convinced than ever about the need for Christian contact with the rough youngsters of our area, and if it was

60

difficult that was no reason to give up. I realised, too, that in expecting dramatic conversions I was trying to tell God what to do. Our responsibility was to preserve faithfully with what needed to be done, and to leave the rest to Him. It still amazes me that He could use us despite our lack of experience and proper understanding of the estate kids, but our very inadequacy meant complete dependence on Him.

I'd long since stopped wondering whether any of the lads would come to church when three of them turned up one Sunday morning and caught our attention by waving wildly from the back pew. We squashed up beside them and tried to look nonchalant as loud whispers ensued, and several curious heads turned round to see what was going on. We were euphoric. The fact that they'd bothered to come at all thrilled us, and although they didn't come back for a few Sundays they appeared from time to time after that. We knew nothing would normally drag them along so they must have really wanted to come, and we prayed that curiosity and novelty would eventually make way for a real openness to God's presence in those services.

Over lunch that day I confessed to Sue that I might have given up long ago if it wasn't for her. Without her support, my confidence would probably have ebbed away completely. So this was what it was like in practice – being in love. Far more than security, or a wonderful feeling, it was a profound source of strength. It was a discovery we might not have made so soon if we had not been faced with such a test of our resources.

I don't think I'd ever had so many different roles to play at one time in my life before. During the day, I was a sober professional in the City. At weekends I was either a handyman around the house or trying to get alongside aggressive youngsters. The Sunday evening youth group continued to go well and Sue and I felt very much at home there, but in the midst of all this activity we were still getting used to each other and finding out what marriage was all about. Every so often I wanted to escape and get right away from all the pressures and demands of other people. Our regular Sunday morning forays in the Kent countryside became a lifeline.

We'd get up early and jump into our convertible Hillman to speed through the sleeping suburbs. Once we'd spotted a field or corner of a wood or grassy bank by a stream that took our fancy, we'd stop and cook our breakfast. Bacon tasted excellent fried on our little portable cooker and eaten to the sound of birds or the wind lazily rippling through the trees. Then we'd walk hand in hand and often without saying much, just letting the fresh air and exercise renew us.

Sometimes I felt guilty about escaping like this and enjoying it so much, but I had to admit my need for such a break, and felt better equipped to get stuck back into things afterwards. Even Jesus sought quiet places away from needy people, and doubtless He appreciated those precious times too.

It was tempting to think just because I felt at home in the country that I was meant to be there and that suburbia and city life just wasn't 'me'. But even as the thought crossed my mind I knew I was simply leaning to the easier option, and there was no reason for God to go for that. Still, at the back of my mind, there was a creeping doubt that I would be a chartered accountant for ever.

As our first wedding anniversary approached, we were as wrapped up in each other and our church activities as ever. We were happy together and didn't seek the company of others particularly since we saw plenty of people as it was anyway. We had a nodding acquaintance with some of our neighbours, but it was clear many of them didn't quite know what to make of us: a young couple, in an area predominantly inhabited by families or older people more established in their jobs and life style, who spent an unusual amount of time at the local church and entertained unsavoury-looking youngsters in leather jackets and heavy boots.

The man next door kindly lent me his lawn-mower in

the spring when our grass had grown embarrassingly high, but the only people we got to know quite well were the family across the road. Howard helped me clear a blocked drain, and I discovered he was the father of the lad with whom I had hilarious bicycle races up and down the street. No better introduction was needed, and Howard, Tim and Jocelyn became firm friends.

We finally knew we'd never get beyond the cool tolerance – very generous in the circumstances – of our neighbours with the lawn-mower, when a hot summer's day gave rise to a very unfortunate incident. The lads had been enjoying their fish and chips in the garden with us, and on the way out had been stopped by the sight of a hose lying innocently on our neighbour's front lawn. Maybe it was the Jaguar parked in the drive that provoked them, but the temptation proved too much. Before we realised what was happening, a jet of water was being directed through the open front window of our neighbour's living-room, and we were the ones left to do all the explaining. How I envied the gleeful escape of our mischievous friends.

Eighteen months after we were married, I passed my exams and qualified as an accountant. The ups and downs of our early life in Orpington seemed to have largely smoothed out, and we felt quite settled in our suburban home. Had we realised what interruption lay ahead to this hard-won state of affairs we might have tried to put off the moment for just a little longer.

4

'When are you going to start a family?'

Sue's father's question was completely unexpected. It was a Sunday afternoon at her parents' home and she had her arms deep in the washing-up while Dr Young dried the dishes and stacked them away.

'He just popped it into the conversation,' Sue told me later. 'I didn't really know what to say.'

It was a beautiful day and we were just on the point of going off for a breath of sea air and a long walk. The thought of children was far from Sue's mind.

'I ... well, we thought we'd wait until Max got his exams,' she began in answer, but as she spoke she remembered that the brown envelope with the good news had arrived some weeks previously. That particular condition had been fulfilled without our really having noticed.

Dr Young continued to dry the plates thoughtfully.

'We'll start a family before too long I expect,' Sue went on, 'but there does seem so much to do at the moment.'

Dr Young understood. 'It's always that way,' he agreed. 'We have a hundred and one calls on our time, especially if we are taking our responsibilities as Christians seriously.'

'Yes – that's just it. The youth work is really busy, what with the kids coming round to see us when they want to. That's so exciting you know, Dad.' Sue swung round to face her father, enthusiasm lighting her eyes, and he laughed.

'Sue, it's marvellous what you are doing and you must

carry on as long as it seems right, but you know having children is exciting, too. They certainly add a new dimension to marriage.'

'Well yes, of course. It's just that – with so much on our plates at the moment it doesn't really seem the right time to start a family.'

'There never is a right time,' was the reply.

All this was related to me in the car on the way home that evening.

'It's really up to us, isn't it?' I said, feeling slightly annoyed at such plain speaking from Dr Young and sympathising with Sue who had clearly been on the defensive with her father. The truth was, the subject of children just hadn't come up recently. We'd been so involved with everything else, we hadn't been thinking about starting a family. It was a happy whirl of activity, but perhaps, after all, it was time to take stock and make a decision.

Sue said it first. 'Shall we think about it, anyway?'

'Fine by me.' I couldn't help wondering what we might be letting ourselves in for.

So, babies became a serious topic of conversation between us over the next few weeks. A subject for prayer too, because we wanted our decision to be right before God and to seek His guidance. If we were doubtful about when to start a family, we were all the more concerned to find assurance from God of His perfect timing.

Our busy church life would clearly have to change with a child around the place. Almost every evening was taken up. There was the Bible study, the committee meeting for the youth group, preparation for the talks, not to mention those times when the kids from the youth group or the coffee bar dropped round to see us. And the weekends of course were used to the full. Sue had even started helping with the local Crusader class on Sunday afternoons.

We'd have to cut down on at least some of these commitments, but the youth work was a particular concern. Some real friendships had developed over the last months, and we suddenly worried that these would be jeopardised if we couldn't invest time in them in the same way. So much patience had been required to get this far with the youngsters from the estate. Would it be a failure of responsibility before God to allow ourselves to be distracted at this stage? And the Sunday evening youth group was thriving and growing. We were needed there and it was work we felt God had called us to do.

The more we puzzled at it, the more we went back to Sue's words to her father. It just didn't seem the right time to start a family.

We prayed about all the young people regularly, bringing their concerns and problems before the Lord and asking Him to lead and encourage them as well as help us to know how best to support them, and it was during one of these times of prayer that something came home to me.

'Sue,' I ventured when we'd finished praying. She was getting up and I reached for her hand. 'Don't make the coffee just yet. I want to ask you something.' At once she was close to me again, attentive.

'We've just been praying that God will bless Alan and George and the others, but do you think we are really trusting Him to do that?'

'Why, yes.'

'*Really* trusting Him, I mean.'

Sue was quiet, waiting for me to go on.

'I know we commit them to Him regularly, but if we were trusting completely that He would look after them we wouldn't be so concerned about possibly spending less time with them if a baby came along.'

Sue nodded slowly.

'If God can work in their lives as He has been doing when we're around, He can do it when we're not. Can't He?'

'Ye-es.'

'Maybe He will find someone else to do it.'

Silence.

'You mean,' Sue said at last, 'that we've been thinking

we're indispensable to them all, when we're not.'

'Well, not consciously thinking that. But getting muddled about our priorities. What's important is not that we continue to be involved, but that God continues to work.'

'Yes.' Sue was more definite now. Together, we bent our heads in prayer once again, asking the Lord's forgiveness from full hearts for letting ourselves place a wrong emphasis on our own personal involvement in the youth work. We gave each and every one of those young people back to God, releasing them into His care completely.

Nothing immediately changed. Our attitude was different, though, and we were ready to be guided in a different direction if this was God's plan.

There was something else that bothered us as we contemplated bringing children into the world. What did the future hold for the next generation? The newspaper headlines were bold and ominous. The nuclear threat had seemed just a speck on the horizon, but now it loomed ever nearer and made us tremble when we thought about it seriously. Violence was on the increase, and moral values and restraint seemed thrown to the winds. Statistics revealed a steady decline of belief in God, and con- sequently in living by His standards. Could it possibly be our responsibility not to cast a child of ours on to such a world?

It was our practice every morning before the day got underway to read the Bible together and pray. We used Scripture Union daily Bible reading notes to guide our study and we had experienced how God could use these times to direct us to a particular biblical truth we needed to hear. Just when we were struggling with the idea that we probably couldn't promise our children much of a future, God stepped in to reassure us through His Word.

We were reading in the Old Testament about how God led the Israelites out of Eygpt and journeyed with them to the land He had promised them. They certainly didn't have an easy time of it, and neither did God as He watched His children not only suffering but becoming discouraged and turning away from Him. Their journey was a long one, fraught with danger, but what we could see from our vantage point as we read was that God was there and could always be trusted. And God was the same yesterday, today and for ever.

'I wonder when in history it might have seemed a good time to have children?' Sue commented. 'I expect there'd always have been something to worry people if they'd thought about it.'

The Bible showed God's people at war and coping with apparent disaster time and again. It didn't mean everyone stopped having children. There had always been wars and rumours of wars. There was evil in every generation. People had suffered and others had prospered.

'Do not worry about tomorrow,' Jesus said, 'for tomorrow will worry about itself. Each day has trouble enough of its own.'

Jesus's prayer for His 'family' was not that they should be taken out of the world, but rather that they be kept from its evil (John 17: 15). We needed to trust God for the future as we trusted Him for each day and for every concern, small or large. So we lifted to Him our family and the children we might have. We pledged our trust in Him for any difficult times that might lie ahead. We reminded ourselves that no matter how frightening the world might seem, God was in control and we could rely whole-heartedly on Him.

That left just one final concern.

'Sue, I'm happy with just us.'

We were walking on one of our treasured Sunday morning outings and I was breaking a companionable silence.

'So am I,' was Sue's prompt reply.

'We'll never be able to race off together wherever we please when there are children around,' I continued.

'No.'

'And I'm not at all sure I could cope with tripping over

68

nappy buckets everywhere and sleepless nights.'

Sue's laughter echoed round my ears.

'There must be something in it,' she said with a twinkle in her eyes. 'Otherwise no one would rave about the joys of family life, would they?'

To be honest, I hadn't come across many children. There were several at church, and occasionally their noise of crying would disturb my concentration, but I hadn't otherwise taken a lot of notice. My main observation was that the moment children came on the scene, their parents would immediately become the rather harassed receptacles for toys and nappy bags and an almost permanent look of exhaustion. I couldn't imagine what it would be like to have a child of my own.

For Sue, it would mean giving up her job as a teacher. She'd been working part-time at a girls' private school near by, having wanted to make good use of her time and qualifications once the house was straight. It hadn't been easy to start with, since she hadn't had any formal training, but she enjoyed the work and clearly won the respect of the teachers. They tried to encourage her to work full-time, but Sue drew the line at that.

'I wouldn't have time for the house or you or anything,' she said firmly. 'That's not what we agreed to begin with, and I still feel our home must be my priority. And if children come along I want to be with them anyway, so it's no good thinking about making more of a career out of my teaching.'

Sue's teaching had also provided a welcome supplement to my meagre income, but now I was qualified we could manage on my earnings. Sue's mind was already on the idea of stopping the teaching, so this didn't pose a problem for us as we contemplated starting a family.

It took the visit of some old friends to clinch our decision. They brought their baby daughter, Fiona, and as they rolled up in their rather rusty Morris Minor estate car, I decided there was another drawback to having children. It seemed to mean getting a sensible, boring car. Driving interesting cars had always given me great pleasure, and I thought fondly of our recently-purchased MG as I welcomed Hugh and Liz. They emerged from the car complete with yellow plastic rattle, naked pink dolly and Fiona, cuddled shyly into her mother's shoulder.

It was a lovely day so we sat in the garden. The others chatted together and caught up on news, but I was increasingly mesmerised by Fiona. The bright-coloured flowers caused chortles of delight, and eventually Fiona was making her way back across the lawn with her prize. A series of soft pats on her mother's leg obtained the desired attention and Liz leant down and smiled with approval at the lovely flower held out to her. The next minute she was apologising to me.

'I hope she hasn't spoiled the plant. The trouble is she loves flowers.'

Concern for my fuchsia hadn't even entered my head. I was actually thinking what else might entertain our little guest. I reached back towards a yellow snapdragon, picked it and held it out to Fiona. She looked at it wonderingly.

'Here you are, it's for you.'

Her eyes jumped to my face, and then back again to the brightly-coloured flower. Deciding she would trust me after all, she stretched out a chubby hand and tried to grab my gift.

'Whoops.' I bent over to where it had fallen, but Fiona was already scrambling to pick it up and finally held it out to me in triumph and with a big smile on her face. That was the moment I saw parenthood could be fun!

'Okay, I'm beaten,' I said to Sue when our guests had gone. 'Let's give it a try.'

We'd concentrated so hard on making a careful and responsible decision that we hadn't really considered the other possibility – that we might not be able to have children at all. We knew there was no guarantee. We knew that even if all was well we might have to wait a long time. In the end, we were in God's hands, and, as it happened, we didn't have to confront these issues because Sue conceived quite quickly.

She made her announcement in February and in a typical fashion. She had – 'in faith' she confessed afterwards – already given up her job, since the end of the autumn term coincided with a long audit scheduled for me in Gloucestershire, and seemed to mark a natural break. I never relished being away from home and Susie for any length of time, so if an opportunity came up for Sue to travel with me I was eager to snap it up. My mother was living in a wing of a lovely Cotswold house only thirty miles from the plastics factory where I was to be based, so we arranged to stay with her, returning to Orpington and our church activities at the weekends.

Our stay was almost over, and as I drove home from work I was looking forward to a last walk in the unspoiled Cotswold countryside and an evening by Mum's roaring log fire. Sue was at the door to meet me, already dressed warmly in her coat and wellington boots.

'Want a quick walk before tea?'

I needed no second bidding, and we were soon striding into the dusk of the evening.

'How was your day?' Sue asked brightly.

Now I had got to know very well the different ways in which Sue might ask this question. Her tone of voice betrayed whether she really wanted to listen to what I'd been doing or whether she was bursting to tell me something herself but held back out of consideration for me. I answered briefly, and then teased her to get on and tell me what was making her so excited.

'How do you always know?' she giggled.

But I couldn't have anticipated the news that she might be pregnant. I came to an abrupt halt and asked her several times whether she was sure and whether she was all right and what on earth were we supposed to do next?

'Am I meant to wait on you hand and foot and treat you like a princess?'

Neither of us really knew.

We had booked a skiing holiday for the following month, and there was much serious discussion as to whether we should now give it up. We consulted the doctor back in Orpington and he seemed to think all would be well if Sue avoided 'strenuous physical exertion', so we decided I should ski alone while Sue limited herself to walking. The doctor might not have given his consent so willingly if he'd realised that a walk to Sue meant anything but a gentle stroll. I was rather horrified myself to come back from a morning's skiing to discover she had already covered thirteen miles!

We came back to a wet English spring. Sue had apparently suffered no ill effects from the holiday, so life continued much as normal.

'Aren't you supposed to develop a craving for strawberries or something?' I asked when Sue had refused a coffee for the umpteenth time and pronounced it all the baby's fault. She'd gone off apples too, which was unheard of until then. Usually she consumed quantities of both.

'Well, carrots taste great at the moment.'

Carrots! I didn't argue. They were easier to come by – and cheaper – than strawberries.

We were full of thanks to God for the tiny new life that was growing day by day. We started thinking about painting the room that was going to be the baby's, and looking out for some suitable furniture when we passed our favourite junk-shop in Orpington. We hadn't yet taken any steps towards stopping the youth work, although Susie inevitably hadn't been able to play such an active role. There was no question of my carrying on without her.

'We wanted to do everything together, remember?' Sue looked anxious, as if she thought I might continue with the youth work on my own. 'And you'll want to spend time with the baby, too.'

'I don't want to do it without you,' I reassured her. 'We're in this new thing together anyway, and I want to be right there beside you.' I took her hand, but her eyes were still troubled. Was it a mother's instinct? Was Sue's strange fear a premonition, as if she knew our togetherness was going to be threatened when the baby came along?

But neither of us could see into the future.

Having trusted the Lord so completely for the ongoing work with the young people, we were given a real jolt soon after our skiing holiday when Christopher Barnes and his wife Freda interrupted our evening meal.

'Oh dear,' the curate apologised as I ushered him into the kitchen. 'Sorry to be a nuisance when you're eating, but Freda and I wanted to let you know our news before the rumours became rife.'

Christopher told us in confidence about his impending move to another church where he'd been appointed vicar.

'I'm delighted about it of course, but ...' He frowned. 'You'll be left with a gap in the leadership here which I know you can well do without.'

I was stunned. The baby was on its way. How could we possibly manage without Christopher? We'd be needed more than ever in the youth group, but that was the opposite of what we'd planned and trusted God for.

Sue was saying how much we'd miss Christopher and Freda and I hoped they hadn't noticed my bewilderment. We should certainly miss their friendship, never mind anything else, and I found my voice to say so.

'But it's marvellous news for you. Congratulations.'

Christopher beamed with pleasure and I wished I could really share his gladness. 'The move had to come sooner or later,' Freda reflected. 'And you'll be pleased to know the vicar is already looking for another curate. All being well he should find a replacement quite quickly.'

That seemed unlikely, knowing how long these things could take, and I complained bitterly to God once our friends had gone that I didn't understand what He was doing.

It took several days for me to accept the situation and admit that we needed God's help more than ever. My trust in Him over the timing of the baby had been shown up in all its frailty, and once more we were challenged to hold on to our confidence in God, whatever things might seem.

'We'd love you to find a new curate quickly, Lord,' prayed Sue.

As before, our Bible reading notes were very appropriate. They directed us to passages in the Bible where God was looking for a leader, and the people He chose were often the least likely ones and the timing completely unexpected. Yet it was always just the right person and just the right time. Who would have thought the young David, just a boy, would kill Goliath and become one of the most famous and powerful leaders in history? And a child left to float in a basket on the River Nile to escape death at the hand of Pharaoh – God had a very special plan for Moses.

God knew what He was doing, and we took heart.

Even appreciating all over again what a great God we served, we still could hardly believe it when we heard that Struan Dunn had been appointed to replace Christopher – and in record time. We should be free to withdraw from the youth work gradually.

Our local paper had started to publish a different country walk each week, and each Saturday would see us folding the relevant page into an anorak pocket and disappearing for an afternoon of exploring. One particular day we had followed the route as usual, winding round Knole Park and through the village of Godden Green, and then setting out across the fields on a public footpath. It was cold and drizzly, and by the time we got back to the car we were tired and looking forward to a warm relaxing bath.

I was getting dressed when Sue appeared, flushed and very worried.

'I think I'm losing the baby.'

Within half an hour the doctor had given orders for Sue to rest in bed for a month and chided me for letting her walk ten miles, get soaked to the skin and then take a hot bath. I was furious with myself. How could we possibly have allowed ourselves to think we could continue as we'd always done? Sue was carrying a precious new life. Hadn't the enormity of that fact got home to us yet?

With a new sense of responsibility at being a potential parent, I invested in several child-care books so Susie and I could inform ourselves better about what was going on and what we should and shouldn't do. I was engrossed in the first chapter of one entitled *The New Childbirth* on the train to London Bridge when I experienced that uncomfortable feeling of being watched. Sure enough, a quick glance round the carriage confirmed my suspicion. Several pairs of eyes reverted sheepishly to their newspapers. My face burned. That evening I hunted through our bookshelves for a book of identical size to the child-care book, and a few strips of sticky tape secured the disguise. *Keats' Selected Poems* now apparently occupied my attention on the train, and I read undisturbed.

Sue hated being confined to bed. She read all the baby books from cover to cover while I fussed and fumbled my way round the household chores in between dashing to and from work. At the end of the month's enforced rest, she cautiously got out of bed and took up her former routine – very slowly and carefully. The doctor kept a close eye on her and gave her strict instructions not to lift anything heavy, so I still had to occupy myself with saucepans and bundles of washing. Really, I was rather enjoying it all.

'Sit down, Susie,' I'd say a dozen times a day. While every so often she would protest, I could see that she basked in this increased attention and concern for her health. Our natural optimism that all would be well bounced back. Sue had a record of excellent health, and no one in her family had had problems with pregnancy or childbirth as far as we knew. There was no reason to suppose the baby wouldn't develop normally and be born safely.

Our new-found confidence was shattered one evening when three lads from the coffee bar descended on us with cheerful 'Hellos'. One of them asked if I could give him anything to do over the next few days.

'Needs keeping out of mischief,' commented his friend across the table.

'Aren't you at work then, Robert?' I asked.

'Doctor says a few days off. Got German measles, haven't I?'

Before I could sympathise or make any suggestions, Sue shot up from her seat at the table and rushed out of the kitchen. Excusing myself from the boys, I followed her into the sitting-room where I found her white-faced and trembling.

'Susie, my love, are you all right?'

'German measles,' she said. 'Robert's got German measles.'

The full force of the words hit me with sudden and sickening clarity. Of course. German measles could cause a child to be born deformed. The page of one of the books where we'd read about it all flashed into my mind. Contact with the disease wasn't dangerous if the pregnant mother had already had it or had been immunised.

'You haven't had it, have you?' I asked, taking her hands. She looked at me with fear in her eyes and shook her head.

She'd had no injection either.

'Sit down here a minute, my love, and I'll phone the doctor.' My voice was steady for her sake, but inside I was praying there was something we could do. Sue sank into a chair, and hung her head miserably. Her whole body was shaking, although it was a warm May evening, and it was then I remembered Robert had been with us earlier in the week, too.

The doctor was encouraging but honest with us. 'A gammaglobulin injection is the only thing I can recommend. I'm afraid it's not foolproof, but they think it can have some effect.'

An hour later we were at the clinic in Maidstone and a syringe needle was being plunged into Sue's arm.

'It may do some good,' the doctor commented noncommittally as he completed the injection. 'You'll just have to wait and see.'

It was late into the night when we drove home. Sue had stopped shaking, but was still pale. We felt bleak and comfortless. The doctor had told us that if Sue developed German measles, we should have grounds for terminating the pregnancy if we wished.

Before we slept that night we knelt beside our bed and committed the situation to the Lord. We felt so muddled we didn't know what to pray for but simply gave the whole situation to Him and asked for His help.

It was a few days before we could talk about the possibility of abortion.

'It would be wrong to kill the baby,' Sue said firmly.

'My love, you haven't developed any symptoms. It might not come to that at all.'

'But Max it *might*. We've got to decide what we should do.'

There was no doubt in my mind that it would be wrong to take the situation into our own hands and terminate a life.

'God gave us this baby after all, didn't He?' Sue went on. 'He's entrusted it to us. A life is still a life even if – if it's born without all its faculties.' Her voice broke. 'Max,' she cried, 'how ever could we cope with a handicapped baby? We'd all be so sad. It would be so difficult. The poor thing would never ...'

'Sue, darling, we don't know what it would be like do we? How can we tell? We don't know what having a normal baby would be like either, and we've had to trust God about that. So we have to trust God in this, too.' I was saying words I believed in my head, knowing we had no choice before God but to accept whatever He allowed to happen, but in my heart I felt the same turmoil as Sue. She was rocking herself backwards and forwards with her arms folded protectively over her stomach.

'We prayed for this baby, didn't we?' I prompted gently. She nodded. 'We were thrilled when we knew you were pregnant.' Another nod. 'God let us keep the baby after we charged round Knole Park in the rain.' This time a shadow of a smile crossed Susie's face. 'So,' I finished carefully, 'I think we must remind ourselves that God is still in control and knows what He is doing.'

We were silent for a long minute, each grappling with competing emotions.

'Right, we've decided,' Sue said at last. 'If I develop the measles, I still go through with the pregnancy.'

We prayed for that unborn life. Whether normal or handicapped, it was God's child and we pledged ourselves to trust in His care for it. We asked for grace to accept whatever gift the Lord gave us, and we prayed for peace. We determined that we should leave the issue alone from then on, and asked God to take away the cloud that hung heavily over us.

He did, and daily we rested in the secure knowledge that God had His hand on events. Sue didn't develop any symptoms, but we knew this wasn't conclusive. We'd been told that it was possible that Sue might contract a mild form of the disease which wouldn't necessarily be apparent.

We felt closer to each other than ever. The journey towards parenthood was being undertaken together. We were united in our apprehension, and in our excitement. We prayed regularly for the little life that was growing. I continued to practise domesticity, and Sue carefully attended to the changing needs of her body. She tired easily, and no longer required cajoling to go to bed and rest.

She was also noticeably changing shape. If I'm honest, I didn't really like Sue's new look. Her face was alight with joy and anticipation, yes, but her shape rather put me off.

Sue startled me by tackling this one head-on in her characteristically forthright fashion.

'Max, you don't like how I look now I'm pregnant, do you?'

'I – er, well ...'

78

'You don't have to pretend. I can tell.'

'Sue – it's not that I don't like it exactly. It's different.' I didn't know how to be honest without hurting her feelings and underneath the confident 'let's have it in the open' manner, I could hear a plea for reassurance.

'Oh, I don't like it much either, you know,' Sue went on bravely. 'I hate having to be so careful all the time.'

'But you've got me playing the chivalrous knight and seeing to your every need.'

She softened. 'Yes, I like that.'

'Well I like it too. I like being able to pamper you and show you I love you.'

She looked at me, understanding.

I loved her whatever she looked like, and explaining it to her enabled me to grasp the truth of it better, too.

'But you still don't like me fat,' she persisted maddeningly. This time I could be honest, because it really didn't matter.

'Well you do look rather funny,' I conceded.

Sue giggled. 'Mmmm. And I waddle like a duck,' and to prove the point she did a demonstration and we were soon in fits of laughter.

As the day drew near, we grew tense with a mixture of excitement and apprehension.

'You'll be there when the baby is born, won't you?' Sue urged.

'Well – yes of course,' I said, covering up my slight hesitation with what I hoped sounded like enthusiastic agreement.

'Max, don't you want to?'

I was stuck for a reply once more. 'Yes, I do,' I said categorically, 'but I just don't know if I'll manage.'

'It's me who'll be doing all the work,' Sue countered, unimpressed.

'That's just it. I can't bear the thought of seeing you in all that pain.'

'I'll be okay if you're there to hold my hand.'

The baby was due on a Sunday, and all day we

anticipated the start of the contractions. Nothing happened. We could have gone further afield for our breath of fresh air after all. Sue practised her breathing exercises, and I tried to control my nervousness at the imminence of what would surely be one of the most important moments of our lives. I fervently wished I knew more about the whole procedure of the birth. They ought to have antenatal classes for men, I thought.

It was two weeks before anything started to happen. By then, we were patiently resigned to the fact that we couldn't time this important event to our own convenience. The contractions seemed like a miracle in themselves, and by the time we reached the hospital they were coming fast and regularly. I couldn't understand why all the staff seemed so unconcerned. Sue clutched my hand, and I appealed to the nurses to come and help.

'The baby must be almost here,' I insisted desperately.

'Don't worry. It will be some time yet.'

Sue's pain increased. She seemed transported into a world of her own, totally absorbed with the effort to bring a new life into the world.

At last I could bear it no longer and grabbed the nurse who was passing our door. It seemed an age since someone had looked in to check that all was well. I was taken seriously this time. The nurse swung into action and soon several white-coated forms were bustling efficiently round the bed, making confident, encouraging noises to Sue.

A moment of pure joy and amazement as the baby made its appearance. A piercing cry. A split-second assessment that she was normal, that she was a girl.

'Thank you, Lord, thank you, Lord,' whispered Sue.

Naomi Joy had entered our world, and would change it completely.

5

How proud I was to be a father. A father! I could hardly believe it. The wriggling bundle I raced upstairs to contemplate every day when I got home from work was really my daughter. If she was asleep, I marvelled at each perfect, tiny feature of her face, the tiny hand clenched beside her, the soft hair that covered her head like down. I was teased at the office for having bags under my eyes and a seemingly permanent grin. The colour of the world had changed overnight. It was bright and fresh and new, revolving around Naomi Joy.

'Had another sleepless night, then?' was a frequent question when I stifled yet another yawn. Often my colleagues were too busy or preoccupied to take much notice of how everyone else was getting on, but the advent of a baby was a phenomenon many of them understood only too well.

' 'Fraid so. Two o'clock I think it was last night, and then she was yelling again at five for her next feed.' Another yawn interrupted my explanation, much to the amusement of my audience. 'I don't suppose they realise at that age how much sleep parents need.'

But I didn't mind really. It was all an adventure, a novelty. Sue and I didn't notice our tiredness. It was all part of a natural process we embraced gladly.

It was a delight when Naomi began to laugh at my tickling her. Before, she just used to scrunch up her toes and fingers and occasionally lunge a kick or two in my direction as a protest. Her laughter was catching and everything else was forgotten during those precious moments – whether it was a train to catch to my next audit or a pan Sue had left on the stove. We were simply caught up in the antics of our daughter, and often spent ages just watching her. She seemed to change a little every day and Sue always had something new to tell me when I came back from the office.

I wasn't very good at changing nappies, but, if the truth be known, Sue looked after most of the baby's needs in those early days. She took to motherhood as if she'd been practising all her life, and slipped easily into the routine of feeding and bathing and changing and rocking and feeding again.

It was a full-time job, and there was understandably little energy left for other things, but I imagined this was normal for the first few months and that it would change as Naomi got older. That was my first mistake.

There was another big change on the horizon as regards my job. It had all been decided and agreed before the baby was born.

The idea of applying for a transfer had come to me when I was driving home late after several days away on a long audit. I was feeling very cross that so much of my home and church life was being eaten into now that I was qualified. I was expected to work long hours in the office, too, and while I managed to draw a sensible line at that for the most part, I could tell it wasn't quite the done thing. I'd already decided I couldn't give heart, soul and everything else besides to my job, so it was infuriating to feel this pressure – and particularly to see the work building up. I turned a corner fairly wildly as I asked myself whether I should be considering leaving, but that was pretty crazy since I'd just spent so much time and effort getting qualified.

A transfer seemed an obvious solution. The company had offices round the world, and the demands of the work would surely be less outside London. Africa maybe ... All that space, and it would be such fun and a marvellous change for us both. The baby would have arrived by then and wasn't an outdoor life supposed to be just the thing for children?

I began to build castles in the air.

When I told Susie, she was as enthusiastic as I was, so I put in my application.

I might not have got an interview let alone a job, but supposing there was a vacancy abroad for me there would still be one other hurdle to negotiate. Peat Marwick normally only paid expenses on two-year contracts abroad, and my contract had only one more year to run. Would I be able to commit myself to another one – even if I wanted to – or would my expenses be paid just for the year?

I didn't mention this until the interview I'd been called for was almost over. It was for a job in Nairobi, Kenya, and the starting date was the following February. To my delight, I was offered the post.

The moment had come, and tentatively I explained my problem.

'Well. I'm sure we can do something about that,' the partner said genially. 'Yes, I think we could make an exception to our normal practice. We'll pay your expenses for a one-year contract if that's what you want.'

So it was all arranged and, at Christmas, two months after Naomi was born, I walked out of our office in the City for the last time. It wasn't with the lightness of step I'd imagined, however. Sue had taken me completely by surprise a few days earlier.

'Max, I hate to bring this up, but do you think we're wise to rush off to somewhere as remote as Africa now that we've got Naomi to think of?'

'What?' I thought I hadn't heard her properly.

Sue repeated what she'd said.

'You mean you don't want to go?' I asked incredulously.

'I'd love to go, you know I would. I'm just a bit worried about Naomi.'

'But Sue, we're supposed to be going in two months. I had no idea you were having doubts.'

'I know. I'm sorry Max. To begin with I thought I was just being silly and that I'd be enthusiastic again sooner or later. But I still feel like staying here and not uprooting to go thousands of miles away.'

I wasn't very sympathetic. We were too far along the road to turn back now, and I couldn't see any reason for Sue's misgivings. 'Your ambition was always to be a missionary in Africa before we were married,' I reminded her. 'You used to talk about pioneering in new places, living in a mud hut with no running water and helping primitive people. You said it was in your family's blood. What's happened to all that?'

'I don't know,' Sue said, miserably. 'I don't really understand myself. I just feel different since I've had the baby.'

As if to put her own point across at this crucial moment, Naomi let out a wail from upstairs and Sue cast me a despairing glance before disappearing to comfort our daughter.

Later, when I felt more rational, we resumed the conversation and Sue agreed that it was going to be very difficult to change our plans at this stage. She'd probably love it when she got there, she assured me, and I wasn't to mind if she worried a bit during the weeks of preparation.

'Susie, darling.' I felt contrite. 'I don't want you to worry.' Perhaps after all it would be better to cancel everything and stay.

'Well, I don't seem to be able to help it. It must all be part of motherhood.' Sue shrugged and set her chin in a gesture of determination. 'I'm sure it'll be all right. I'll just have to keep a careful eye out for Naomi.'

She didn't raise the matter again and neither did I, relieved that she seemed to have come to terms with the move. I was puzzled by her new instinct for settling down and feathering a protective nest for Naomi, but didn't dwell on it. There was too much to do.

Had I made more effort to understand I might have been better prepared for what lay ahead. I was still operating under the illusion that a child around the place doesn't change things that much.

January was a whirl of activity. I busied myself with arranging for our luggage to be transported ahead of us and organising the details of our own journey. Among a hundred and one other things, I had to sell the car and find a home for the cat. Sue seemed increasingly preoccupied with Naomi, and I found myself longing for the times of closeness and sharing we had enjoyed before the baby was born. Our early morning picnics were a rare luxury now, and with our other activities similarly curtailed we seemed to find almost no time even to talk. Either there was a predictable interruption from Naomi, or we were simply too tired or preoccupied with our own thoughts. I consoled myself with Sue's words that everything would be fine when we got to Nairobi. Once the hectic period of moving was over and we were settled into our new home, things would surely get back to normal.

Africa! It was another world and stunningly beautiful. So much open space stretching for mile upon mile. It was like the fulfilment of a dream, and I felt as if I'd shed all the pressures and dirt of London like a skin that had grown too tight. The relief was enormous.

The vastness of the country was broken by scrub, or trees shaped like African combs, or the bright-coloured garments of the African tribeswomen. The air was so fresh it seemed that my lungs were swept clean with every breath. The days were scorchingly hot, the sun searing the streets and buildings of Nairobi into a bleached haze. Cotton clothing was all we could stand to wear, and frequently we needed to change more than once a day. The nights were cooler and filled with a thousand sounds that beat together like the pulse of Africa – crickets, insects, unidentifiable stirrings that were all part of the living land that never seemed to sleep.

We rented a bungalow on the northern outskirts of Nairobi in the district of Kabete. Some of the streets of the city were broad and tree-lined, with showers of red and purple bougainvillia spilling brightly over the pavements. Others were narrow, unkempt dirt-roads full of potholes. Wealthy African, Asian and European businessmen and their families lived in gracious, comfortable homes set back from the wide streets, while the poorer people found shelter in shanty-town dwellings. I suppose such a dual society is to be found in every major city the world over, but it seemed particularly noticeable to us in Nairobi, perhaps because everything was so new and different. Every day we encountered the city's poor, standing on a street corner begging and in rags, or sitting propped against a building in the shade, head bowed.

Our home was simple, and furnished with items we found through the local paper. Its best feature was a wonderful view over twenty miles to the Ngong hills. Sue and I loved it.

We'd barely been in the country a few days, when we made an appalling discovery. It seemed that every European family in Nairobi had at least one servant, and we were both rather shocked when we realised the same was expected of us.

'Max, we can't employ someone to do things for us when we could very well do them ourselves,' Sue protested. 'Just because all the others have African servants doesn't mean we have to.'

Neither of us felt comfortable with the idea of having people waiting on us, and to us the employment of black people seemed little other than the promotion of the racial divide we could see so clearly around us.

'Don't you find the heat draining? You'll be glad of some help, you'll see,' we were told. It was true that even after such a short time we were missing the English 'nip in the air', but we hadn't found it difficult to adjust to the heat and couldn't see how this justified giving all the household chores to someone else.

But there was another side to the question – the issue of unemployment, and this was the deciding factor. We quickly understood that the less educated black people desperately needed to find employment, and working for Europeans was perhaps their only chance of an education and status. The alternative might be no work and no income, and once we realised this, we understood our responsibility. Gradually, we came round to the idea of employing someone to help Sue in the house and someone to do the garden.

'But we must make them feel as much at home as possible,' insisted Sue. 'We'll teach them all we can and treat them as equals. Don't you agree?'

'Wholeheartedly.'

So Jane Wahu and Luka Omari came to join our family. Jane was in her late teens, full of shy smiles and knowing nothing about keeping house or looking after a baby. Sue had to teach her from scratch, but she was soon devoted to Naomi and never anything but supremely gentle and responsible with her.

Luka was a quiet, tall man with a shining ebony face and immensely strong. Our garden wasn't elaborate, but he worked in it loyally. He embarrassed me, too, by insisting on always calling me 'Master'.

We did none the less achieve a level of friendship. Both Luka and Jane came with us to the Baptist church we'd started attending, and after a while Luka surprised me by asking me to tell him about Jesus. Apparently, his parents had been converted by missionaries and Luka himself had once been an active believer, but had rebelled in his teens.

'Max, did you know Luka's parents have prayed for *years* for him to be employed by Christian people?' Sue's eyes shone with excitement when she told me this. 'Yes, really. Isn't it amazing the way the Lord works?'

Once Luka had broached the subject, we often talked together about the Lord, and his openness and genuine desire to learn was a tonic after the battleground of the coffee bar. A real bond was established between us through these conversations.

Another tonic we discovered in Africa was the wildlife.

Although some kinds of animals roamed freely throughout Kenya, the game parks were the places to see the full and fascinating variety of African wildlife.

There was something magical about going into these special reserves and watching the animals in their natural habitat. We'd drive slowly along the dust tracks, laughing at the cheek of the monkeys who came to sit on the car bonnet and at the easily-frightened zebra who fled from our path in waves of black and white movement. Many of the other animals seemed unconcerned at our arrival, and when the car was stationary they took no notice of us at all.

A real treat was to discover a pride of lions, lazing sleepily in the shade of thorn trees after feeding on their kill. Hyenas would hover on the side-lines waiting to pick up the remaining morsels once the lions had moved on, and every movement of the protagonists in this drama held us enthralled.

Nairobi National Park was just outside the city, and it drew me like a magnet. Time and again, I'd urge Sue to join me and we'd either pop Naomi into her carry-cot and hope she'd sleep in the back of the car, or ask Jane to look after her.

'We won't be long,' Sue often said as we waved goodbye to Jane, and I found myself wishing she could relax from the demands of the baby and just enjoy the game park for as long as possible. That certainly wasn't easy if Naomi was with us. Before we'd driven any length of time or seen very much at all, the telltale murmurs and restless noises would start from the back seat. We'd both try to ignore them, but when the real crying started and Sue became more and more distracted from the beauty around her, I knew we'd have to head for home. Sometimes I did it before Sue asked me, but increasingly I tried to block out the baby's unhappiness and squeeze as much enjoyment as possible out of being in the game park. Sue's eventual plea that it was time to go often met with a resigned silence as I turned the car around.

Even when Naomi wasn't with us, Sue was alert to her needs and became restless as feeding time drew near or she felt we'd been away too long.

Much as we both loved the open spaces and freshness of Africa, and didn't regret for a moment our decision to come, there was a strange unease between us. I didn't admit it for a long time. Perhaps I preferred to believe it wasn't there.

'Let's go away for the weekend,' I suggested on a quiet evening when I thought I would burst if I didn't get out into the country around us that was just waiting to be explored.

'Go away? Where?'

'We could treat ourselves to a couple of nights in one of the lodges in the Masai Mara game reserve. You know we've said we'll do it one day – well, why not now?'

Sue looked doubtful.

'But it's expensive, Max.'

'Yes, I know, but we can afford it just this once. We could both do with a real break.'

'What about Naomi?'

I'd decided it would be better if Naomi didn't come, otherwise there would be all the usual distractions.

'We can leave her with Jane.'

'Max, you know we can't do that. I'm still feeding her myself.'

I wrestled with my feelings. If the option was to go, taking Naomi with us, or to give up the whole idea, the choice was clear.

'All right. Let's bring Naomi, too. A family weekend.'

Sue sighed. 'It's a lovely idea, but I don't think it's on really. Not yet, anyway. Naomi is still very young and we'd have to take so much stuff with us – nappies and everything.'

I was cross by now. It had seemed such a good idea. The others at the office were always coming back from weekends in the game parks and telling me of all that they'd seen and done. It didn't seem too much of an ordeal for them. Why should it for Susie? I was sure we'd manage perfectly, nappies and all.

The silence continued and I could tell Sue wasn't going to change her mind. She looked tired.

'Right. We'll go to the National Park for an hour or so then, shall we? Perhaps on Saturday.' Sue didn't seem to notice my tone of undisguised disappointment and gave me a quick hug.

'That would be lovely. We'll go to the Mara another time.'

The next day, Naomi was up and bright as a button when I got home from work. The telephone was ringing and Sue handed the baby to me on her way to answer it. I still loved to play with her, and as she gurgled and squealed with delight I asked myself how I could possibly have wanted to go away and leave her for a whole weekend. It was as if we were linked by an invisible thread. It was as strong as the toughest cord when I held her, but became perilously thin and even insignificant when she was out of sight and I was busy with all the other demands of life.

Later that night, when Naomi wouldn't stop crying and Sue and I were robbed of any sleep we might have got, I wished I was going away on my own. Anything just to get away and have some peace and quiet. And yet Sue and I had pledged never to do things apart from one another, wanting to preserve our togetherness.

But what togetherness did we have at the moment?

I was horrified at my own thoughts.

I'd been wanting to buy a really good camera to take photographs of the animals, and with the prospect of going into the game park that Saturday I decided to make my purchase. I wasn't sure that my funds could stretch to a camera of the quality I really would have preferred, but was delighted to discover that the prices were far lower than they would have been in England. I came out of the shop with a Pentax single lens reflex, complete with interchangeable lenses, and carried it home with pride.

'I hope we see something worth while in the park,' I said excitedly to Sue. 'I can't wait to try this out.'

We set off on Saturday with slightly false brightness. There was a truce between us, and also a sort of pledge. We each wanted to please the other, yet held firmly to our own points of view. We'd only go so far. But inasmuch as this expedition represented a step towards each other it was important, and we didn't want it to be spoiled.

After an hour in the game park, we'd relaxed. My camera was whizzing, catching animal after animal in its frame – zebra, water buffalo, ostrich. I was quite content to photograph all the familiar sights and not to worry about the rarities which seemed to be elusive that morning. Sue eagerly pointed out flashes of movement in the distance and seemed really to be enjoying herself.

Then I caught sight of a flurry of yellow birds settling just up ahead of us on the road. I had no idea what they were and reached for my bird book.

'Do you see them? Such a bright yellow.' I flicked through the pages and then put the book down impatiently. I had to get close to photograph them before it was too late.

My hand was on the key to start the car when Sue ventured that it was getting late and almost time for Naomi's next feed.

I don't know why it all burst out at that moment, but it did. I exploded. I shouted furiously at Sue that she was always out to spoil my enjoyment, that she'd lost all her sense of fun and adventure.

'And you're obsessed with the baby.'

I could hear the anger hitting Sue as if I'd struck her physically, and inside I recoiled from the pain I knew I was inflicting. All my vague and bottled-up feelings of the last few weeks crystallised suddenly and ruthlessly. And worse still, once the lid was off, the sense of injustice I'd barely acknowledged not only declared itself but seemed entirely warranted.

Why shouldn't I have a hobby? I fumed silently as I drove far too fast in the direction of home. Can't I enjoy myself? Perhaps after all I shall plan the odd expedition on my own. Why on earth not?

'Sue, I'm sorry,' I said, much later.

'That's all right,' in a quiet, tight voice.

'Really – I don't know what got into me. I – I didn't mean to hurt you like that.'

A pause. 'I know,' and Sue reached out to clasp my hand, then to hug me silently and tightly.

Two days later I was driving home from a visit to one of my clients. I was earlier than usual, and as I passed near the game park I felt its irresistible draw and looked at my watch. Over an hour to go before Susie would expect me home. There was time to pop into the park and take some photos. Sue didn't even need to know.

It was a blissful hour. The sun glowed richly on the broad expanse of land and the slow-moving river in front of me. I watched the lazy crocodiles sunning themselves and then slipping into the murky, cool water, and I experimented with different settings on my camera as I took several pictures.

With a start, I remembered Sue would be waiting and hastily checked the time. Not too late. I locked the camera in the glove compartment and drove home. I didn't say a word about where I'd been. Sue was cheerful and not too tired, and we were laughing about something halfway through the meal when I found myself almost telling her about the crocodiles. A pang of guilt stopped me, and then I was annoyed about feeling guilty at all. What did it matter if I had been into the reserve without Sue? I was entitled to some time to myself after all. I'd enjoyed it, and would look for another opportunity to do the same again.

Keeping my enjoyment to myself wasn't the same as sharing it with someone, especially with my best friend. I could still tell her. But I kept it quiet.

Over the following few weeks, there were several opportunities to spend time in the reserve and I got through a lot of film. At work during the day I'd wait impatiently for my time to be my own. Things certainly weren't as busy in Nairobi as they had been in London, and I would often be free before the afternoon was over if I'd been out visiting a client. Ironically, I missed the stimulus of the London office. It was all very well having more energy when I got home in the evening, but what was there to do with it? Instead of the glow I used to feel when I got home and spent precious time with Susie, I began to resent being tied to staying in one place when I wanted to go out. The baby took up as much of Sue's time and attention as ever, and the strange distance between us seemed to be getting wider and more difficult to cross. My visits to the animals became more than just an indulgence, they became a release and I saw them as almost a necessity for my peace of mind.

Just occasionally, as I sat in the car on my own, I acknowledged that the satisfaction I found in watching and photographing the animals was really only surface deep. Always, deep down, there was the guilt that I was deceiving Sue and the recognition that I was making the distance between us worse at the same time as I lamented it. But I always pushed these thoughts away if ever they surfaced, and told myself again that I was perfectly justified in doing my own thing and that Sue would only be hurt if she knew I was coming into the game park without her, so it was better to keep quiet.

One day I lost track of time and Susie startled me as I pulled the car into the drive. She came running out of the house.

'Max, darling, where have you been? I was worried you'd had an accident.'

'Oh – er, sorry. Am I late?'

'You're nearly an hour late. Is everything all right?'

'Oh, I should have phoned, I'm sorry,' I stalled, desperately trying to think what I could say. I studied my brief-case. 'I – I had to stay late at McKenzie's. The staff couldn't agree the trial balance.'

Fumbling, I locked up the car and told Susie I'd hurry to get changed for supper. I dashed into the house.

Safely inside the bedroom, I caught sight of my face in the mirror. 'You liar!' I accused my reflection and turned away, unable to meet my own eyes. I was trembling. What on earth was I doing? Intending to enjoy myself I'd woven a web of deceit and now I'd told a blatant lie. I was caught in a trap of my own making and hated myself.

I changed and went out on the veranda where Susie was arranging the table. I decided I had to tell her what I'd been doing.

Conversation over the meal was stilted and eventually I put down my knife and fork and tried to find words to explain. It came out in a jumble – how I couldn't adjust to her preoccupation with the baby and resented her lack of attention to me, how the game park had been a solace, but that I'd deliberately kept my visits a secret from her in a crazy bid for independence and my right to enjoy myself.

Sue had stopped eating and the pain and bewilderment on her face spurred me to hurry and tell her everything, everything. There must be nothing left to separate us any more.

At last I finished. I'd apologised, but it seemed so pathetic a gesture after so wilfully breaking the trust that was between us. It seemed then as if we might never find it again, as if Sue might never forgive me.

I was haunted for weeks by what I'd done. I'd shattered our ideals, betrayed the spirit of our charter. I'd been unfaithful to Sue. She'd been shocked and upset, but had told me at the end of that dreadful evening that she forgave me. I could see she felt she had to do that, but I couldn't take it as real. I couldn't accept her forgiveness because I couldn't forgive myself.

'It's partly my fault, Max. I shouldn't have been so inflexible. I didn't realise you were feeling so shut in and unhappy.'

To begin with I felt worse as Sue tried to take some of the blame on to her own shoulders. I now couldn't see it had

94

anything to do with her, forgetting how unloved I'd felt. It was all my fault. It took a while for me to appreciate that we'd both contributed to it, but eventually we both became more objective and saw things in their proper perspective. Distance lent consolation. There was no excuse – I could never excuse what I had done – but we understood better what had happened and why. We reached out to one another again.

But I felt helpless as I tried to look into the future. How could we make our relationship strong again and defend ourselves from any more such shattering failures?

Our faith was very battered and small, but we had nowhere to turn other than towards God, and we prayed that He would give us the help we so badly needed. We asked Him to infuse new life into our relationship and new attitudes into our hearts. I was at a loss to see how it could happen, but I held on to the knowledge that God could do it.

A deep, unexpected fear still gripped me. Suppose we didn't sort it out? Suppose we were too different to live happily together? We were only 22 when we got married after all. How could we really have known each other?

Such doubts had begun to nag at me during my clandestine visits to the game parks. They were so new and disturbing that I tried to blank them out of my thoughts, but persistently they came back. Perhaps I was simply more of an adventurous type than Sue. Her own instincts seemed to lean much more to the home and a settled family life, and motherhood had brought them out in their true colours. Were we going to be travelling different paths from now on?

I couldn't get beyond that terrible question.

'Max – what are you thinking? You've been very quiet this evening.'

I was jolted back to Sue's presence beside me on the veranda where we'd been sitting, watching a beautiful, fiery sunset. I didn't want to share what had been going through my mind. It amounted almost to a vote of no confidence in our relationship.

'Oh, nothing much.'

Sue didn't let it rest there. 'Please tell me.' I knew how difficult she found it when I kept my feelings to myself, and she must have sensed there was something important behind my silence this time. She was trying not to let any barrier creep up between us again, and I didn't want that to happen either.

'I was thinking about what makes people suited to one another.'

'You mean us, for instance?' This came back so quickly I wondered if Sue could see into my thoughts.

'Well – yes.' I took a deep breath. 'Do you think we're compatible?'

At first Sue insisted that we were. Hadn't everyone said so when we got married, and hadn't we got a million things in common? What made me think we might not be?

'We are compatible in some things, but not everything,' I said carefully. 'Perhaps it's only now that the differences are surfacing.'

Sue opened her mouth as if to protest again, but then checked herself. She acknowledged there were differences and that, yes, they did bother her. 'But we're married and that's that. We'll have to work it out.'

So simple. And yet where did we start?

It seemed obvious really, but we'd never considered whether the Bible actually gave advice on what to do when a relationship hit a rough patch. We knew it had plenty to say about building the relationship, but what if it was falling apart? Did God have anything to say then?

We decided we should devote an hour each evening to a concerted search of the Scriptures. We'd prayed that God would put love back into our relationship, but if there was something we could and should do ourselves we wanted to know about it. I had never thought seriously about whether the Bible addressed issues of incompatibility or lack of love in a relationship for the simple reason that I had never imagined I would be facing them myself.

'. . . love comes from God,' says 1 John 4: 7. 'Everyone who loves has been born of God and knows God. Whoever does not love does not know God because God is love.'

The passage was familiar to both of us, but for the first time we applied it to the specific context of our marriage.

I realised that love was fundamentally nothing to do with how I felt, or how well I got on with someone. It was to do with my relationship with God. If I wasn't being loving, I couldn't blame my circumstances or the fact that the woman I'd married had apparently developed some irritating habits and so made me feel less tender towards her. It wasn't that I was falling out of love with Susie. I'd had a misguided idea of love in the first place. 'Whoever does not love does not know God . . .'

The idea that I might have been failing both in my responsibilities towards Susie and towards God was hard to take, and this was only the first discovery I made as we began our Scripture search. At each painful realisation, we had to come consciously and humbly before God in prayer, asking Him to go on teaching us the truths of His Word and to give us courage to try and understand and face them.

It was far from easy. There were times when I wanted to run away – anywhere. It was just too much to struggle with the exacting commands of the Bible when I sometimes wondered if we'd ever be strong enough really to put them into practice.

There was some assurance in Galatians. If left to their own devices, human relationships would descend into discord, jealousy, selfishness and 'fits of rage' (5: 20). We laughed ruefully together. We certainly weren't up against anything unusual. Realising that a loving relationship could lose all warmth and even become one of hatred was actually a relief to us. It wasn't that in our case things were particularly wrong. Without God, we would inevitably suffer the consequences of our humanity, but with Him, as Galatians highlighted, relationships could be transformed: 'the fruit of the Spirit is love, joy, peace, patience, kindness, goodness, faithfulness, gentleness and self-control' (5: 22–3). The qualities we longed for in our marriage weren't things we could manufacture ourselves but the result of Christ's presence with us.

But we had prayed and sought to follow Christ closely throughout our marriage. Perhaps less so during the difficult weeks just recently, but in general we had tried to be obedient to His commands. What was missing? What more could we do?

Even as I struggled with this, it was as if God removed another layer of blindness from my eyes.

He had already revealed that a lack of love in any relationship couldn't be attributed to external circumstances. What about when things were going well? By the same token, it couldn't be because I'd just behaved in the right kind of way. I couldn't take credit for the good times any more than I could blame for the bad ones.

But I'd always wanted to think I could manage myself and my affairs and my marriage, and if they seemed a little rocky at any time, never mind. Eventually I'd find a way to sort it out. And if God could help, well, so much the better.

It seemed as if God was making me see now that I had to surrender completely any right I thought I had over my life and particularly over my marriage. Paul didn't let the Galatians think it would be easy to enjoy the fruit of the Spirit in their lives. 'Those who belong to Christ Jesus have crucified the sinful nature with its passions and desires' (5: 24).

Crucified. Put to death. Renounced all rights.

I searched myself. Had I done that? If I'd thought I had, I'd been mistaken. How many times had I urged people to come to Christ because he was longing to set them free and to fill their lives with joy and peace? Had I not preached about the cost because I was only dimly aware of it myself?

God was teaching me some hard lessons. Crucifixion couldn't be anything other than a painful process, but as I studied the passage in Galatians it came home to me powerfully that I couldn't hope to step into the new dimension Christ offered without surrendering my old way of doing things. There was little chance of a new dimension in my marriage to Susie without a real acceptance that only God could bring it about. I had to step down and give Him room.

It was one thing to recognise the need, but quite another to act on it.

'If you love me you will obey what I command' (John 14: 15), Jesus said to His disciples. As I looked at this verse I thought of Peter, the apostle who'd boasted he'd stand by Jesus whatever happened, and yet denied Him when things got rough and he was afraid. When Jesus was being crucified by His angry opponents, Peter claimed three times never to have known Him. Three times, when He had gloriously risen from the dead and come to be among His friends, Jesus asked Peter if he loved Him. And three times, Peter said that he did. Jesus had known about Peter's remorse at his failure, and wanted to restore him. Like Peter, despite everything, I knew that my love for God was the most important thing in my whole life.

But if I love Him, John's Gospel revealed, it should be demonstrated in action. I should obey His commands.

It was late in the evening some weeks after we'd begun our study when I came to this point. Susie was sitting in the chair opposite on the veranda, but we hadn't spoken for a long time. God had different things to say to each of us. I prayed to Him silently. I echoed Peter's words – Lord, you know that I love you. You know I want to obey your commands. I am willing to crucify that part of myself that is selfish and gets in the way of your purposes but – and my shoulders drooped lower in the chair as I confessed my fears to the Lord – it's so hard. And I'm afraid I'll fail like I've done before.

'Whoever has my commands and obeys them he is the one who loves me. He who loves me will be loved by my Father and I too will love him and show myself to him' (John 14: 21). My eyes were on the chapter once again, and the verse leapt out as if spoken directly from God to my heart. It wasn't a question of my struggling alone. As I endeavoured to draw closer to God, so He would draw close to me. It was a two-way relationship. That first step was possibly the hardest, the step away from self and old securities. But once it was made it was easier to see that the way ahead was not beyond endurance because God would be there and ever closer with each new step taken.

For the first time for what seemed months, thankfulness and praise bubbled up within me.

We really only saw the change when we looked back. It didn't happen obviously or quickly, but instead of feeling frustrated at having to come home in the evenings I was glad to get back. I found myself once again wanting to spend time with Sue. We sought out some new things we could do together and enjoyed games of tennis, a drive-in cinema we'd found near by and even some weekend trips to game reserves.

Our morning time of prayer and Bible reading, which had become strained and dull during the months of my deceit, came alive again. And we continued our practice of picking up our Bibles in the evenings when there was time. What had begun as a desperate search for help had become a journey of increasing excitement as God reassured and encouraged us through His Word. Love was deliberate and practical, and the more we understood this the more we saw that it was within our capacity – however demanding it might be. Not only that, but as we tried to put into practice what God was teaching us about biblical love, the precious flame of attraction was fanned to life between us once more. We'd thought compatibility was the foundation of our marriage, and that we were inevitably headed for disaster without it. But once we'd got our feet on the real and firmer foundation of God's love and provision, it was as if He gave back our old happiness together.

Other things happened. We were invited to run the services at the Children's Church in the Lavington area of

Nairobi. It was an idyllic-looking timber church set in a beautiful garden where the young people from two boarding-schools met at the crack of dawn every Sunday to worship God. We would have been uncertain about taking on such a responsibility when we were each feeling insecure and unhappy, but we now saw it as an opportunity to do something we both enjoyed and work at it together. We accepted enthusiastically, and threw ourselves into organising the services and making friends among the children with increasing delight. We had barbecued breakfasts together after the service, and often played hilarious and exhausting games of volleyball.

Then we received an invitation to speak and sing at a school Christian Union. The only problem was that the school was situated some distance from Nairobi, and I envisaged Sue worrying about Naomi and reluctant to let me go on my own.

'We must go,' insisted Sue to my astonishment. 'They've taken the trouble to invite us. We can't let them down.' So we went, taking Naomi in her Moses basket and fitting feeds and nappy changes into spare moments.

When I stopped to think about just how much Sue had to do each day to keep Naomi happy and well cared for, I felt ashamed at my resentment of her preoccupation. How could I expect her to have as much time for me as I'd been used to before the baby was born? I remembered the sacrifices I'd gladly made when Sue was pregnant. I'd been wrong to relax into my old habits. With a pang of conscience, I realised I'd been acting for all the world as if there hadn't been a new addition to the family. It was time I grew up! I began to make a much more conscious effort to be a proper dad and the more time I spent with my daughter and with her mother, too, the more I realised with enormous relief that it wasn't all sacrifice. The early days of euphoria at being a father didn't seem so distant after all.

The first time after our argument that Sue admitted to

being too tired to come with me on another photography expedition, she was quick to add that I should go on my own.

'Susie, darling.' I shook my head. 'I'd far rather you were with me.' And I meant it. I was amazed that my attitude had changed so radically in such a short time. But Sue insisted.

'Max, I really don't mind, you know. I don't feel so possessive of you.' She laughed. 'I know you'll come back!'

And strangely – or perhaps not so strangely – I felt less inclined to go off on my own as Sue minded less about my doing so.

My adventurous craving to explore the further riches of Africa persisted none the less, and Sue gave me her blessing to explore Murchison Falls in Uganda and also to go up Mount Kenya. Neither expedition was without incident and both were among the most memorable events of my whole life.

Climbing Mount Kenya meant three days away from home. I spent the coldest night of my life in sub-zero temperatures at 15,000 feet, battled with mountain sickness and narrowly escaped death by exposure. Not that I put it quite like that when I told Susie all about it afterwards, but if I hadn't been feeling unwell at the summit with the classic symptoms of mountain sickness I might have agreed to go down by a different route chosen by two of the friends I was with.

'That often happens,' the mountain rescue chief told me at the end of the afternoon when my friends still had not made it back to base and I went to report my concern.

'What do you mean?'

'People make a change of plan at the summit, but the lack of oxygen and high altitudes can affect their judgment. I've known some think they could fly to the moon! It's always wiser to plan your route in advance and stick to it.'

The rescue team returned at midnight, long after the warm sun had given way to icy cold temperatures and I'd begun to fear for the lives of my friends. They'd got lost on the way down and on the point of exhaustion had found a mountain hut where the rescue team had discovered them.

In Uganda I encountered a wild elephant – or at least I thought it was wild as I beat a hasty retreat from the creature's huge bulk. I'd seen notices posted all over the hotel where I was staying, warning the clientele about approaching any of the animals in the game park, however tame they might seem. No one had told me the elephants were regular raiders of the hotel dustbins, and it was only when I burst through a door marked 'staff only' in my bid to escape that the truth became evident. My quaking legs and gasps for breath caused the staff considerable amusement.

Sue listened with something approaching horror to both my tales, and was clearly relieved to have me home again. The thought of my running from a tame elephant made her hoot with laughter.

'You are a chump, but I do love you.'

I can't remember exactly when I realised the fear that had gripped me so icily had gone. We were happy together. Our love wasn't the same as before, but was deeper – older and wiser perhaps. We'd discovered that human love was fallible, but that God's love could put the broken pieces back together into something stronger.

'Sue, I've got it.' I shouted triumphantly from our sunny living-room one Saturday morning. Naomi was clutching my fingers tightly in an effort to stay upright on her two sturdy legs.

'What?' Sue's voice echoed from the kitchen and the next minute she popped her head round the door.

'I've decided there's no such thing as incompatibility.'

Sue looked suitably surprised at this pronouncement, and then amused.

'Well, that's good. So you won't mind if I spend this afternoon in the garden instead of going to the game park after all.'

Naomi teetered as I let go one hand to grab a cushion.

Then she plopped down heavily on to her nappy and watched in surprise as I threw my missile at Sue. I missed.

6

Even as we were feeling more settled and happy in Nairobi, God was preparing the way for change.

A school speaking engagement was coming up, and I was busy one evening working out what I was going to say. Susie wasn't going to accompany me since the school was a good forty miles away, but she no longer minded the thought of my going on my own.

I was excited as I anticipated the event. What could be more satisfying than sharing the good news of Jesus with a group of people, and knowing the Spirit could touch the hearts of the listeners and draw them to God?

In fact I wasn't just going to be speaking to one school but to three. Children from two other schools were coming over to join pupils of the largest school in the area, which boasted a grand assembly hall to accommodate everyone. I watched in amazement as the hall filled up. By midday, about 300 youngsters had gathered, their faces alight with joy and enthusiasm as they raised their voices in choruses of praise. I sat rather uncomfortably on the platform, marvelling at the exuberance of the singing and thinking that my talk would probably be hopelessly inadequate. Clearly these people had tasted already the goodness and love of God.

A small, crumpled piece of blue notepaper was handed to me. It was the programme.

First event: We have one hour singing and testimonies.

Second event: Mr Max Sinclair will speak one and a half hours.

Third event: More songs and testimonies.

I hope no one saw me gulp as I read how long I was expected to speak. One and a half hours! What a change from the twenty-minute or half-hour slot I was used to in England – longer than that and people would start to get restless or look at their watches. But I'd already learnt that time had a different value in Africa. When the singing eventually came to a stop I detected a certain reluctance, as if everyone could have gone on happily, but attention was quickly focused on those who were giving testimonies. The audience nodded and smiled and clapped spontaneously, and then it was my turn.

I'm not sure that I have subsequently been guilty of failing to fill my allocated speaking time, but on this occasion I fell short. Not that anyone seemed to mind, since the singing was once again taken up with enthusiasm and afterwards a number of people graciously commented how encouraged they had been. I shook dozens of hands and answered eager questions, but one young man approached me with serious eyes and a serious enquiry. Would I help him to become a Christian? As I spoke and prayed with James Maginda I felt the familiar thrill of God's family and His kingdom being extended.

James was the first of many young Africans I encountered who committed their lives to Christ. There was a great hunger to learn and an openness among these people, and it was a privilege to take up opportunities to speak and share my own experience. In retrospect I can see that God was confirming my calling to full-time evangelism long before I ever saw it as such, or came to the point of being willing to set out on the path He was preparing for me and the family. It was as an evangelist that I felt thrillingly at one with myself and the Lord. He'd put an evangelist's blood in my veins and although the full implications of this were not yet clear, it wasn't long before God started to point us more specifically in this direction.

The first hint came with the post from home. My cousin, Justyn Rees, was running Hildenborough Hall in Kent, a Christian conference centre that was engaged in evangelism. Sue and I had helped once or twice on the youth weekends before coming out to Kenya, and Justyn surprised us by suggesting that we might like to join the staff. At that stage, preparations for our move abroad were already well underway and there was no specific guidance from God that we were meant to change our plans. So we'd declined, and come out to Kenya as planned. Justyn wrote regularly about how the work at Hildenborough was developing and how exciting it all was, and again extended his invitation for us to come and join him. He did it disturbingly often.

'J is now saying there's an important job for us back at the Hall and he's praying about it a lot,' I informed Sue as I scanned the latest letter.

'Well, perhaps we'd better think about it.'

I was surprised. 'Sue, you're not saying we should leave Africa?'

She laughed at my dismay. 'No, no. At least, not exactly. But if poor J is feeling this so strongly we ought to take a bit of notice, don't you think? And, anyway, the fact that we'd rather not consider it probably means we ought to – if you know what I mean.'

'But I don't want to go back.'

'I *know*. Neither do I. But that's not what I mean.'

So we thought about it, and the more we thought the more we wanted to stay. We'd settled into a very happy routine and loved Africa. Not only was it a beautiful country to be in, but there were so many opportunities to share our faith and we couldn't see how God might be leading us to give up those. Only the other day we'd been asked to speak on radio and TV on a programme that would go out at Christmas and give the Christian message. The invitations from the schools were still coming in and our youth work at the church was flourishing.

There was another consideration. Africa was a marvellous environment for children and we'd dreamed of our family growing up in its wide open spaces. Sue was newly pregnant with our second child.

We agreed that we needed some very specific guidance from God. We asked Him to intervene and show us if He wanted us to go back to England, trusting that He wouldn't let us make a mistake.

One of the crucial factors in the whole dilemma was, of course, my job. My contract in Nairobi had been for only a year, and was therefore due to run out before much longer. If we were to stay in Kenya, I had to make a decision anyway, and this was quite independent of the new factor in the equation – Hildenborough. I could apply for an extension to my contract or look for another job in accounting.

'Or I could do both,' I thought aloud to Sue.

Whatever I did, the result would tell me whether or not God intended me to carry on with my career in accountancy.

So I decided to investigate an extension to my present contract and also to push the doors of possible alternative jobs. If one of those doors opened and the way seemed clear to stay in Kenya, we should take that as a sign from God of His will. If they closed, however, we should know that He had different plans for us.

The first step was to chat with the senior partner of Peat Marwick in Nairobi. He had already hinted that he would be willing to extend my contract if I wanted to stay, and he confirmed as much at our meeting. He also offered me a generous increase in salary.

So that particular door stood open.

Stage two was to pick up contact with a previous client who had been very appreciative of the help I'd been able to give. There was a reorganisation of the accounts department in the offing and he'd told me there might be a job going. I was to let him know if I was interested. Now the opportunity had come to take him up and I telephoned. Yes, the job was still open – would I come and talk it over? It all sounded very positive, and providing the general board agreed to the scheme I was assured the job would be mine.

The next development was quite a surprise. The telephone rang at home one evening and the man at the other end introduced himself in a very well-spoken English voice as the chairman of an international chemical company. The company needed a new chief accountant to handle their operations in Kenya.

'We'd like to invite you to consider the position.'

I hadn't even pushed that door!

I went along to the interview the following week having firmly resolved on the approach I would take, provided the job appealed to me. I reckoned the company could afford to pay me well, so I would request a substantial salary. If such terms were met I could be pretty sure I was meant to be in the job. It was another fleece.

My terms were accepted.

So, I had three options, and each looked very promising. Of them all, I was drawn most to the job with the chemical company. It had just the right challenge without threatening to be so demanding that it would take me away from home with long hours of overtime. A house and a car went with it.

'It seems too good to be true,' Sue said.

I decided to turn down Peat Marwick's offer to extend my contract since the work was not as stimulating as I wanted if I was to commit myself to it for a number of years. Then my old client telephoned me when the board had met and said with regret that the new scheme had not been approved. They were sorry they wouldn't be able to employ me.

That left just one door, the one I might have chosen anyway.

We were on tenterhooks for three or four weeks. There were more meetings and telephone calls, and all the indications were that I should be taken on. I was to be recommended to the full East Africa Board.

When the telephone call came, it was a real shock. The recommendation had been overruled and another man appointed. Sue read my face as I walked back into the kitchen.

'You didn't get it, did you? That means back to England.'

God had answered our prayers very specifically, but it wasn't really in the way we'd hoped. We'd often lamented to each other that dramatic answers to prayer happened more to other people than to us, and here we were feeling numb, not thrilled, in the face of God's clear guidance. For me, it would mean a huge career change, and for Sue a completely new life style to which I would have to adjust as well.

'I'll be able to understand much more about what you're doing.' Sue tried to look on the bright side. 'And even get involved perhaps.'

Once back in England and working with young people in a Christian endeavour, I should surely feel at home and happy. It took a while to get used to the idea, but eventually we felt calmly certain and excited about going back.

Christmas came, and with it the radio and TV broadcast we'd promised to do. Nobody checked my script in advance and so my message about Christ being alive today and able to change our lives and attitudes remained unabridged. Between our songs together, I told our invisible audience that Christ could take away the suspicion and lack of trust between people of different colour and tribe. I extended this to apply to Protestant and Catholic, employer and employed, but what I naively didn't appreciate was that I was encroaching on the taboo subject of tribal conflict in a country where it couldn't have been a more sensitive political issue.

When I explained the gist of the programme to

colleagues at the office the next day I got a very shocked response.

'You didn't really say that! If anyone in the government sees or hears your programme you'll be out of here before your contract is finished.'

So God could have found a much more dramatic and immediate way of getting us back to England! But as it happened there were no recriminations, and instead we were asked to do two more programmes before leaving the country.

I couldn't resist our last opportunity to see Africa.

'Sue, we simply must make the most of this chance to travel,' I pleaded. There was a whole month to spare before I had to be back in England, and since Naomi was older now I felt sure we'd all manage. Sue agreed, and we planned a rather ambitious trip of several thousand miles into the far corners of Kenya and Uganda, taking Jane with us to care for Naomi.

It was a breathtaking experience. Among many other places, we visited Sue's birthplace in the hills above Eldoret, in the north-west of Kenya. Sue's father had built a mission station there, and the hospital he'd designed was still flourishing.

'Come on down into the valley just over there,' Sue urged during our stay. I followed her along the little paths of packed red earth surrounded by acres of lush, green vegetation to a fast-running stream in the crook of the hills.

'There – look! It still works.' It was a wooden water-mill. 'He built it himself.' Sue looked around her nostalgically. 'We used to play for hours round here. We were so happy.' I remembered taking her to my own child-hood haunts when we were on our honeymoon, and was glad now to share her memories as she had shared mine.

The tension in Amin's Uganda was very evident, and we were constantly unnerved by the soldiers we encountered everywhere. We were determined not to let this spoil our enjoyment and so we pursued our itinerary as planned, but I should have realised the toll this would take on Sue and Naomi. Although she started the trip with great enthusiasm, Sue understandably became very tired since she was now several months pregnant. Our little daughter grew increasingly fretful from the heat and long hours in the car, and it began to look as though we ought to go straight back to England once we'd finished this trip. I'd hoped we could stop off in Israel on the way home, since we had an open-ended ticket, but it became clear that Sue and Naomi had had enough.

'Go ahead without us,' suggested Sue. 'We're much better off heading for home, and I can start looking for a house. You can tell me all about Israel when you get back.'

It was too great a temptation to resist, since I'd always wanted to see Israel.

We returned to Nairobi to pack up and say our farewells. The African sun was pouring into the living-room as we knelt with Luka and Jane to commit ourselves once again to God's care, trusting the future to Him. None of us knew what lay ahead, and we drove from the house with lumps in our throats.

Sue and Naomi went straight back to England as planned while I still had one more magical experience to look forward to. Israel was all that I'd dreamed and more. To walk where Jesus walked, feast my eyes on the country He saw daily, visit the places where He preached – it moved me greatly. I saw fishermen on the lake of Galilee, and sat on the shore early in the morning. It was all so real that I wouldn't have been at all surprised to see Jesus and His disciples walking towards me. The New Testament account of Christ's sufferings made me cry as I read it sitting with my back to a gnarled olive tree on the other side of the Kidron valley. It was not the recognised sight of the Garden of Gethsemane, but was more authentic to me.

I missed Sue a lot, often wishing she was there to experience the special atmosphere of Israel. I wondered how I would ever manage to convey it to her, but had no idea just how difficult it would be.

Even as the plane lifted into the air to take me home, I found myself mourning the country I was leaving behind. I didn't want my visit to end, and didn't feel ready to face the family straight away, or all the new responsibilities of Hildenborough Hall.

Sue welcomed me as if I'd been away for years, and eagerly quizzed me about all that I'd been doing. She wasn't prepared for the moody, uncommunicative response she got.

'But you must be able to tell me about the places you visited. What did they look like?'

It suddenly seemed totally unsatisfactory to describe them to her like that. They meant so much more than the bricks and trees and people that made them up. But this was really no more than an excuse since, subconsciously, I was jealously guarding an experience that had been my very own. I'd tasted independence again for the first time since we'd been married, and I was reluctant to let it go.

'It's just very difficult to explain,' I said lamely.

When a bit more time had gone by and I felt settled again, I was able to open up to Sue and tell her about the sights and sounds and smells. I could also see with the benefit of hindsight what had happened. Three weeks wasn't a very long time, but it was the longest time we'd ever spent apart and a salutary lesson as to how quickly we could lose touch with each other. It seemed to confirm that our original instinct to do everything together was right. Of course England would seem drab by comparison with Israel, and it wasn't surprising that I should feel distant from Sue on my return when she hadn't been alongside me during what had turned out to be a very rich and rewarding experience. It hadn't driven a permanent wedge between us, but I was determined not to let it happen again. I resolved to think long and hard before being away from Sue for any extended period.

'Not unless it's absolutely necessary,' I told her.

But I had yet to discover that I didn't need to be miles

away to travel a path that excluded Sue.

Our new home was a wonderful answer to prayer. It was a large, timber-framed house with the untypical name of Pepperland, surrounded by fields and trees and a carpet of bluebells. I could hardly believe it when I first saw it. The country. No noise of traffic or city grime. No suburbia. And Hildenborough Hall was within walking distance – no commuting! It was a dream come true. There was even an old pigsty at the bottom of the garden, which Sue planned to turn into a chicken-run. She'd always wanted to keep chickens and enjoy fresh eggs every day.

With the birth of our new baby imminent, Sue and I decided it would be lovely for her to be delivered at home this time and Anna Mary arrived on July 20th. It was a real family occasion, much more so than it could ever have been in the impersonal environment of a hospital, and Naomi was able to meet her new sister very quickly after she'd entered the world.

'Nice little baby,' was her comment as she peered over the edge of the cot. Anna Mary was clearly a welcome intrusion into her young world and she took to following Sue and the baby everywhere, and was never far away when it came to folding a nappy or holding a tin of baby powder. Even I felt a little more practised in such things the second time round!

There was a lot to do to the house to make it properly habitable and to put our own stamp on it, and I did as much as I could before my new job got underway. I was in my element – knocking down a wall to make a larger living-room area, and remodelling the upstairs accommodation to make two small extra bedrooms. They would be just right for the children. Together, Sue and I designed a warm red-brick fireplace in the living-room and created archways and alcoves.

But it wasn't long before I was totally immersed in the new challenge of life at the Hall, and on a path that would take me farther away from Sue and the girls than I'd ever been before, even in Israel.

From the very first day at Hildenborough, I sensed that God had placed me somewhere very special indeed. I was awed that He should have chosen me to join the very dedicated and faithful team of people who helped to run the conference centre. Discussion on the first morning centred around long-term plans and goals, and culminated in a time of prayer for God to direct every step taken. I sat with my head bowed listening to my new colleagues bringing their hopes and aspirations to God, and appreciated for the first time what a privilege it was to be involved in such work for God. I also realised the great responsibility of the task we set ourselves – to reach out with the good news of Jesus Christ to those who might never have heard it before.

Hildenborough Hall was founded by my uncle, Tom Rees. He saw it as a centre both for evangelism and for refreshment for those who were already Christians. The building he chose for his God-given purpose was a beautiful country home set in acres of Kent countryside, and the peace and presence of God seemed to radiate from every spacious room. Justyn was committed to carrying on what his father had begun and his spirit and zeal were contagious.

'We are in such a privileged position, Max,' he'd told me. 'Here we are in our mid-twenties set free to work for Christ with a ready-made band of prayer supporters who back us to the hilt. What more could we ask?' He had a deep sense of responsibility to those who sacrificed time and money for Hildenborough, and a vision for the work that was undaunted by any obstacle. I listened eagerly as he outlined the responsibilities he wanted me take on: expanding the outreach into secondary schools, making our publicity more imaginative, keeping a tight rein on our finances, and building and training a team of young people who would help us in evangelism.

'When those youngsters stop working with us and go back to their own churches,' continued Justyn, 'they will be able to pass on what they've learnt and encourage others. There's really no limit to what God might be able to do through Hildenborough.'

I felt I had never set out on a task that was more worth while or had such potential. Excitedly, I plunged into my new job with all the energy and commitment I could muster.

I wrote dozens of letters to schools, explaining our purpose of wanting to make the study of religion more lively and relevant, and offered our services for school assemblies, religious-knowledge classes or lunch-time activities. I followed the letters with phone calls, and then drove miles to visit personally each school that responded. Many of the teachers were sympathetic and welcomed the help we could offer on a subject that was clearly difficult and often only included in the curriculum because it was a legal obligation.

I approached churches who might be interested in setting up a mission, and visited clergy and supporters for detailed discussions about how their willingness and commitment could be turned into effective action. Our team was wanted all over the country.

Our team. As I was busy setting up opportunities for outreach, I was also advertising for committed young Christians to join us, interviewing them and watching a talented and enthusiastic group come together. Many were school- or college-leavers who were willing to give a year or so of their time before moving on to something else. Some were musicians, others singers, and others simply wanted to share their faith. We trained them in evangelism, and by the time the first mission came round we'd all reached a high pitch of expectation.

'Perhaps I should do something, too,' Sue ventured as I relayed some of the last-minute arrangements we'd had to squeeze in.

I shook my head emphatically at her suggestion. We'd manage. There were plenty of people with their hands to the wheel. It was just all rather hectic. Once this mission was over, I reassured Sue, things would calm down a bit.

It was wishful thinking and I knew it. Once the first engagement was completed, there was another and another. None of us wanted to slow down, anyway. We were caught up in the thrill and excitement of seeing God work. But I'd missed something behind Sue's words. She wasn't proposing that she join me in the job at the Hall. We'd known Christian couples for whom home and children took a poor second place to the priorities of their work, and we saw this as one of the dangers of full-time Christian work. Sue didn't want to fall into this trap any more than I did. But she was beginning to feel unhappily left out of the new excitement in my life. I didn't realise it, but I'd begun another journey without her.

'Don't try and do absolutely everything,' she said. Her warning fell on deaf ears. I felt I couldn't do too much. The teams were in constant demand and as the months passed hundreds of young people stepped forward to tell us of their commitment to Christ.

It was inevitable as everything developed that I should have to spend a good deal of time away from home. Frequently, two or three nights would be taken up preparing for a mission, and then there was the mission itself when we would all be housed by hospitable members of the church for a week or more at a time. When I was at home, the working day began with a team meeting for prayer at 8.30 a.m., and would go on to be filled with paperwork, phone calls and planning meetings, not to mention training sessions with the teams and rehearsals for music and drama. Although I usually tried to be home for a meal with Sue and the children, I would often be out again afterwards addressing evening meetings or visiting churches in preparation for a mission. Even when I was actually at home the phone would ring and I'd be immediately engaged in making arrangements for some activity or another, or I would have to shut myself away to prepare a talk or learn a new song. The days just weren't long enough.

One March evening I stepped through our front door to

be greeted by a 2½-year-old bundle of energy in her dressing-gown. Naomi flew across the hall from the kitchen and grabbed my knees.

'Daddy, Daddy – we've been waiting.'

I scooped her up and hugged her breathless.

'Don't,' she screeched, laughing. 'You're . . . you're late. Tea's burnt.'

'Ooh dear. Let's go and find it, shall we? I'm hungry.'

The rich smell of an overcooked casserole filled my nostrils as I opened the kitchen door. Never mind, it would still be delicious. Sue was bent over the stove and hardly returned my greetings, and in the dining alcove on the carpet Anna was whimpering unhappily. The children must have been difficult that day. Sue's continuing silence said as much, or so I thought.

'I'm sorry I'm late,' I began, sitting down at the table.

Sue sighed as she put the plates and the casserole on the table, flicking her hair back from her tired and rather flushed face.

'Lots for me,' said Naomi, who had scrambled on to her chair between us. Sue spooned out the meat in silence.

'I had to phone Ken before he went out and didn't have a chance . . .'

'Why don't you say grace so we can all eat,' Sue cut in. Her eyes were fixed on her plate and she didn't look up as she spoke. I decided explanations could wait, and when Naomi was tucking into her food I took the opportunity to try and find out what was upsetting Sue.

'Has it been a hard day with these two?' I kept my voice low so Naomi wouldn't pick up on the conversation.

'Not really,' Sue said quietly. 'I'm cross because you're late. I had this special casserole for you and I particularly asked you this morning if you would be on time. I know it's silly – I'm sorry.'

She looked down at her plate and I thought she was going to cry.

'I was just telling you that I had to phone Ken.' I was bewildered that Sue should mind so much about my lateness. She knew things cropped up at the end of the day even if I was on the point of going out of the door. It was part of the job, and it was important that I met those demands. Surely she appreciated that. I was frowning, but apologised again.

'You said you were sorry yesterday when you had to phone someone,' Sue replied, still in the quietest of voices.

'Yes I know but . . .'

Sue looked up quickly and interrupted me.

'Don't think I'm not glad you're home this week, because I am.' Naomi was still eating hungrily, while our meals went cold on our plates. 'It's just that – well, even though you're here there seem to be so many things taking up your time. You're either at the Hall until late, or preoccupied with it during the evenings – if you're not exhausted. I'm finding it rather hard.' There was an edge to those last words that told me Sue was in fact very angry.

Taken aback, I turned my attention to eating while Sue plunged on.

'You don't seem to have the energy to fix anything around the house let alone the time to sit down and chat. I had to call in a plumber this afternoon. I couldn't stand that faulty tap any longer.'

'You called in a plumber?' I raised my voice and stared at Sue in disbelief. Naomi looked at me, puzzled, and I made an effort to control my reaction while visualising large bills. 'You know we can't afford a plumber,' I hissed. 'I promised to deal with that – I could have done it tonight.'

'You promised that two weeks ago,' Sue was quick to remind me. 'I know it may not be your fault but – well, I wonder if it's right that your work comes before everything.'

'What's for pudding, Mummy?' piped up a small voice, the owner of which had just finished her casserole. Sue bent her face close to Naomi's. 'Ice cream,' she said, and grinned for the first time since I'd come home. 'Pity you don't like it!' Which delighted Naomi, of course, since there was nothing she liked better. 'I do, I do,' she shouted.

Sue glanced at me as she rattled the plates together. 'I don't want to make a fuss. Let's talk about it another time.'

But we avoided the issue – or perhaps I avoided it. I remained firmly convinced that my work was a priority. It was a God-given calling and I needed to give it the best of my time and energy. Perhaps I should be more rigorous about my day off though, I thought. Yes, I should try and make it the same day each week and stick to it. Sue seemed pleased when I told her.

I had another thought. Perhaps if Sue was able to get along to the Hall sometimes she would see what sort of work we were all doing and catch a sense of its importance. And she might feel less left out that way, too, because by this time I was beginning to appreciate that Sue missed very much our joint efforts in Orpington and Nairobi to communicate the Christian faith.

'That's a lovely idea.' Sue's eyes sparkled when I suggested she came along to the Hall the following Friday for the beginning of the youth weekend I was running. She would meet the young people and they could put a face to her name, too.

'I've told them all about you,' I warned her teasingly. 'They'd love to meet you. Most of them are coming from schools we've visited recently and we'll find out what's been happening since we were there.'

There were just over a hundred youngsters booked in for the weekend, and Sue sat fascinated through the introductory chat and nodded enthusiastically at various points during Justyn's short but punchy talk on a passage from the Bible. We went to stand at the back of the lounge at the end of the session. 'What a lovely crowd of people,' Sue whispered, squeezing my hand. 'And you were great at making them all feel at home.'

My head swelled and I was just about to reply when a blonde-haired girl broke away from a group near us and came over.

'Hello, Max,' she smiled, and before I knew what was happening she'd given me a warm hug. 'We had such a good time after you came,' she went on eagerly. 'Do you know the numbers have doubled at the Christian Union now?'

I was thrilled to hear that, but still somewhat embarrassed at her uninhibited greeting in front of Sue.

'Mandy, I'd like you to meet my...'

But she was racing on with more news of the effects of our most recent school mission. I could see she might never include Sue in the conversation and decided there was only one thing for it.

'This is my wife, Sue,' I said firmly. Mandy held out her hand and I hurried on. 'Now I'll leave you two to have a chat if you'll excuse me. I must just see about the music workshop for tomorrow.' And I slipped away.

At about 11.00 p.m. Sue and I made our way home, leaving a crowd of young people in the lounge with their guitars out and singing choruses together.

'What did you think?' I asked Sue eagerly. 'Did you have a good chat with Mandy?'

'Yes – well sort of. She was very friendly and did most of the talking. She said you quite often mentioned me and the children and she felt she knew quite a bit about us already. That was nice – but it felt strange not to know anything at all about her. And I don't suppose I'll ever see her again.'

'Oh, what about Sunday?' I chipped in. 'Bring the girls over for Sunday lunch.' We'd talked about this, too, and although we'd agreed it would be a good idea we hadn't actually put it into practice.

Sue sounded doubtful. 'Well – we'll see.'

It had actually been very hard for Sue to join fleetingly in this one activity at the Hall. There wasn't time for her really to get to know the people, or to get involved properly. Although she'd enjoyed the evening, she was wondering whether short visits could ever be really worth while.

And there was something else.

'Max,' she said later. 'Do many girls hug you like that?'

Her voice was very earnest.

'Only the good-looking blonde ones.'

'No, I'm serious,' Sue persisted. 'Tell me.'

'They are young, exuberant and enthusiastic. A lot of them feel a special link with the teams who have helped them.'

'I felt really strange when Mandy hugged you,' Sue went on pensively. 'I've never met her before in my life and yet she knows you really well. It made me feel quite funny.'

I gathered her up in a big hug to reassure her.

'I didn't realise what glamour there was to your job,' she added, now comfortably resting her head on my shoulder. Glamour? I hadn't thought of it like that.

'There's plenty of grind, too,' I reminded Sue.

'It's almost like you're a kind of mini rock star, up there on that platform.'

That comment hurt, because I enjoyed playing in the band.

'You'll have to watch it or you'll get big-headed, you know.' Sue was grinning, but the seriousness in her voice was unmistakable.

The development of our team work to something much more polished and professional was something I was proud of. I felt we had to attain to the highest standards for God. We now had two music teams, 'Pace' teams as we called them, and they were very competent. The youngsters we visited in schools and churches and those who came to the Hildenborough youth weekends responded to a good band, and I felt they could identify with us better as a result. Once they were relating to us, it was easier to communicate our Christian faith and challenge them with the gospel message. Maybe there was glamour, I mused – but did it matter? It was all for God's greater glory.

I was none the less sufficiently concerned after Sue's comments to suggest that we pray together specifically about the developing ministry at the Hall and the effects it might have on our home life, but there was a very long way to go before I managed to integrate the priorities of my home with those of my work.

The most basic lessons of life are always the hardest to learn and sometimes need going over again and again. In Kenya I'd been side tracked from the needs of my family and my responsibility towards them, and I thought I'd learned my lesson. And yet here I was falling into the same trap all over again. I had no idea that when I was away Sue would pace up and down our sitting-room in anguish. 'He's ignoring me, Lord,' she would burst out. 'And I can't take it. Why won't you make him spend more time at home?'

But I didn't, and Sue had to find her own way of coping with my absence. It wasn't that she couldn't manage. She was admirably capable of running our home single-handed, and perhaps this as much as anything allowed me to remain unaware of my wrong priorities for so long. It was Sue who carved out a garden in the overgrown tangle of bramble that surrounded Pepperland, Sue who did most of the digging in the vegetable patch, Sue who patiently looked after the children. She felt she had no choice but to throw herself wholeheartedly into her own life.

'As I kept myself busy every day,' she confessed to me much later, 'I realised I could survive quite well. That really shook me. I enjoyed doing everything in the end, and wasn't unhappy, but sometimes I was horrified at what was happening. It seemed so wrong that we should be living almost separate lives, and I didn't want to. I wanted us to be together.'

Once, when I'd been away for several days, she came to the Hall with the children to welcome me home. The team van was due at lunch-time, and she thought she'd surprise me instead of waiting for my arrival back at the house.

'I'd washed my hair specially,' she recollected, 'and I think I was even wearing something new. The children were washed and dressed in clean clothes and behaving beautifully – and you didn't notice any of it. You just rushed off with Justyn the moment you arrived, having said a very fleeting hello and not even kissed me. It was awful. I felt like going home and crying for a week, and throwing the meal I'd made you into the dustbin.'

At the time, her unflinching determination to carry on as well as she could and to continue to be supportive of me and the work I was doing, kept her outwardly calm and controlled. She understood the significance of what we were trying to do at the Hall, and didn't in any way want to impede the evangelistic work. It was a dreadful dilemma and Sue's response was to put her head down and get on. She was stalwartly taking what she saw as her responsibilities as a wife and mother very seriously indeed, and I did nothing to ease her dutiful burden. My own duty to the work God had called me to do preoccupied me totally – but I found myself on increasingly shaky ground.

There was never a more crucial time when I needed to seek God prayerfully day by day, but I wasn't doing it. Or at least I wasn't doing it properly. We had times of prayer every day at the Hall, and Sue and I kept up our regular practice of studying and praying together in the mornings, so I was doing a lot of praying really. But, without realising it, I was actually withdrawing from *personally* meeting with God and seeking His view about the tasks and responsibilities before me.

Throughout my Christian life I had sought fellowship with God in prayer, in praise, and in just going about my daily business. In the past, I would often sit down with a hymn-book in front of me or a psalm and simply enjoy praising God in the words of the writer. I talked to the Lord about anything and everything, but now these precious times alone with Him had dried up. I never knew there would come a day when I allowed the fellowship of the Lord's people to be a substitute for fellowship with the Lord Himself, but this was what was happening. It was only a matter of time before even that fellowship became dry and mechanical, and Sue was quick to notice and to comment on it. My pride was stung at her criticism, but since God was continuing to pour out His blessing on the work at the Hall I was distracted from thinking anything was seriously wrong. It was just a bad patch. God knew what was going on and would take care of things. As long as the work continued, I was fulfilling my responsibility.

But the Lord's work had slowly and subtly replaced the Lord of the work as my priority.

I became guilty of double standards – preaching about the necessity of absolute truthfulness and honesty, and yet letting a white lie slip past my lips if it was more convenient that way or paved a smoother path to the attaining of a goal. I was hardly aware of the seriousness of my attitude, somehow convinced that my ministry was important enough to justify these little things that didn't really matter. At home I was giving no more attention than before to the needs of Sue and the children – and a new addition to our family was on the way.

But Sue miscarried.

It happened while I was at the Hall and Naomi and Anna were with me. Sue had been confined to bed for most of the previous five weeks, having been warned she was in danger of losing the baby, so I had taken the other children off her hands as much as I could. She'd been painting a picture in the garden, and it was all over by the time I came home.

I felt terrible – not only because of the death of our unborn child, but because of my neglect of Susie. I told myself it might never have happened if I hadn't left Sue with the many demands of running the home.

Sue was very stoical. 'I suspected it might happen,' she told me through tears. 'All that time I was lying on my back trying to hold on to the baby I knew it didn't want to stay. It's funny, really. Now that it's happened I'm relieved in a way.'

But that didn't change her very real grief for the child we'd lost, any more than it did mine, and we were both thankful to God that He brought us through this period relatively quickly and with few scars.

'There must have been something wrong with the baby,' Sue reasoned. 'I'm sure God wouldn't have let it die otherwise.' We found we could accept what had happened in this way, and prayed that there would be other children to help fill the gap.

When Sue found she was pregnant again, we were thrilled and the birth of Ben was a joy. He seemed an extra special gift after the loss of his older brother or sister, and we both relished the now-familiar routine of seeing to a new baby's needs. Even getting up in the night didn't seem a hardship, and the two girls loved him. The house was filled with laughter, and I was a proud husband and father.

In November 1976 Hildenborough's council of management met as they did every quarter to give advice and take any major decisions. About ten Christian men and women offered invaluable support to Hildenborough's work in this way and on this occasion they agreed that Justyn should take a sabbatical since he had run the Hall for six years.

'We'd like you to take over Max.'

And these words brought me face to face with the very real need for God's help that I had been virtually ignoring over the past months.

In the first instance I felt flattered. I accepted the responsibility for the running of the Hall and directing both the conference centre and the ministry team, and sensed once again the tremendous privilege of such a position.

Then I was on my knees before God confessing my pride and my dismal failure to keep in close fellowship with Him. It was one thing to follow Justyn's lead, but quite another to take the lead myself, and I felt totally inadequate. My helplessness brought me to the throne of Christ as nothing else might have done. I sensed His assurance that He was near even though I felt I had put myself far from Him.

I felt like the blind man whom Jesus had healed by first

putting mud on his eyes and then telling him to go and wash it off. It was as if my vision had been blurred by mud and once it was washed away I could see everything with a clarity that filled my heart with joy.

Prayer was a necessity as I faced my new responsibilities, but it also became a joy. Worship and praise flowed from my deepest being as I sought the help and guidance of God. It was an old lesson that had needed learning afresh: dependence on God brought me into a right relationship with Him. I was freed to be used, and He was given room to work effectively and in power.

I was due to take over the running of the Hall the following April, and realised that my time with Sue and the children would be encroached on even more unless I did something about it in advance. It was clear to me now that I'd allowed myself to become far too wrapped up in my work. I had a responsibility to my family humanly speaking, but also before God, and was guilty of neglecting it in both respects. I determined to be around as much as possible for the children, particularly at bedtimes when we read to them and had a special family prayer time. Sue and I prayed that God would help us maintain His perspective on the work that lay ahead.

Before Justyn went on his leave, we knelt together in Hildenborough's peaceful chapel.

'Lord, you know I need your wisdom to help to run the Hall and to look after Sue and the children,' I prayed fervently. Justyn, with his characteristic large faith, asked God to give me much more than I had sought and to make the months ahead the greatest time of blessing in my life.

Both our prayers were to be answered, but in ways we could not possibly have predicted.

7

I ran the Hall for three months – and it worked. The staff rallied round under my leadership and even seemed keen to put into practice one or two ideas I tentatively suggested. It was exhilarating. I felt more settled in my work there than at any point during the previous five years, and at one with God and my family. Life had never been so good. I began to wonder how things would change when Justyn came back from his sabbatical, and what my role would be then.

I never found out. On July 23rd, 1977, something happened which changed our lives completely.

We were driving back from Devon where we'd been celebrating our tenth anniversary with a group of friends who had got married in the same year. It had been a wonderful evening with a candle-lit meal and all the trimmings. We'd all dressed up for the occasion, and I'd even borrowed a dinner-jacket – it was all very reminiscent of our wedding-day and the Moss Bros. suit! We'd taken Ben with us and left the girls with some friends back at home, but our desire not to be away from them for long meant that when the dawn chorus woke us early on the morning following the party, we decided to get up and start on the return journey. It was just after 5.30 a.m. when we crept out of the still-sleeping house, with Ben drowsily wrapped in his sleeping-bag.

It happened very quickly. Even at that time in the morning the traffic was heavy – it was a holiday weekend and we couldn't have been travelling at more than about

45 mph when I saw the car pull out of the stream of traffic coming in the opposite direction. The horrifying scene played itself out in front of my eyes in slow motion. The car was creeping further and further out of line. I saw it so clearly and yet couldn't believe what was happening. An orange Ford Capri. Suddenly it was directly in our path, and I wrenched the steering-wheel over in a frantic effort to avoid collision. A flash of orange filled the windscreen. Then nothing.*

I woke up slowly. I couldn't remember anything about the crash but the car was at a crazy angle and I was surrounded by jagged metal. My eyes pricked and I saw glass everywhere. The windscreen must have shattered. Susie. Where was she? And Ben?

A confusion of impressions. Squashed feet beneath the accelerator pedal – they were mine. Bloodstained jeans and my hands lifeless in my lap. I tried to turn my head to see if Susie was all right but I couldn't move. There was a searing pain in my neck that threatened to blank out any other sensation. I struggled to stay conscious.

'Max, Max, darling. Are you all right? Max, I'm here, darling.'

Sue was holding one of my hands. I couldn't feel anything. Relief washed over me that she was all right.

'Hold my head up. Please hold my head up.' I couldn't breathe.

Was I dying?

Ben – where was Ben? He was fine. His sleeping-bag had protected him. Nothing but a few cuts and bruises. Someone was looking after him, a very kind lady, Sue said. I realised there were people around the car. In the distance I heard an ambulance siren.

Sue was speaking to me and the words were clear and sweet. Verses from the Bible. However could she remember them so perfectly, and ones that were just what I needed to

* The full story of the accident and its aftermath is told in *Halfway to Heaven*.

hear? Verses of assurance that spoke of God's closeness. It was like being on the threshold of heaven. I could almost see in, and thankfulness that God was calling me home welled up within me. And to be close to the person I loved most in the whole world at such a moment – there was nothing more I could have wanted. There was no terror at the prospect of death, no anguish at the thought of leaving Sue – only peace and total trust in God.

'I love you, Susie.'

'I love you, too.'

The ambulance seemed unnecessary really. I shouldn't need to go to hospital because I was already on a journey of a very different kind. And yet as I was lifted carefully out of the car I thought perhaps God didn't mean me to die just yet after all. Everything was under control now that I was in the capable hands of the ambulance staff. It would be all right.

In fact there were hours of darkness and uncertainty ahead. I had broken my neck. I must have hit my head against the roof of the car as the Ford Capri slammed into us, and it was a wonder the other driver escaped unhurt. He had fallen asleep at the wheel.

It was extraordinary that at the moment when fear and pain might have been at their most destructive, straight after the crash, Sue and I were protected completely. Amazing though it sounds, my physical agony was nothing in comparison to the overwhelming love that filled and surrounded me – love for Sue and her love for me, love for the Lord and His love that seemed almost tangibly real as I lay in the crumpled car. God gave Sue and me His special grace for that moment, and again and again throughout the succeeding days He upheld and comforted us.

I've since thought a lot about the timing of the accident. In so many ways it seems that God graciously prepared us to be able to cope with its horror. If it had happened any sooner, there would have been many things I'd have wanted to sort out before God as I stood at the door of heaven. But the previous few years, and particularly that time at Hildenborough since Justyn had been away, had brought me face to face with a number of things that needed putting right. They'd been dealt with. And in my relationship with Susie – how could we have basked so simply and joyfully in our love for each other if we hadn't drawn close again after our difficulties? If there had still been things unsaid between us, or harboured guilt, I could never have contemplated leaving her and embracing death so calmly.

I was away from home for six months altogether – almost a lifetime in many ways. During the first weeks, I hung perilously between life and death, stripped of everything I'd held dear and taken for granted.

At the most difficult moments of recognition that I might never walk again, God's reassurance was deeper than I can ever remember experiencing. My utter helplessness and the intensity of the pain threw into stark relief the light and love of Christ, and my relationship with Him was my lifeline.

I was eventually transferred to Stoke Mandeville Hospital in Buckinghamshire, the best-known spinal injuries unit in the country. I didn't think much of it at first. Completely exhausted and in fact very ill after one of the worst journeys I'd ever had to endure, I looked out of the ambulance at what seemed to be a collection of huts. I'd thought Stoke Mandeville was a gracious country mansion! My first few days there were bewildering and unhappy, and just when it seemed I was back on the path of recovery I suffered a serious asthmatic attack that took me to the brink of death once more.

It was almost more than Susie could bear. She'd seen me nearly killed in the car crash, then rallying, only to sink back again after the journey to Stoke – and then recover once more. Was this new setback going to be the last? Stunned and fighting back tears, she reached out to God in a desperate prayer, and it was then – in the middle of the day when she never normally slept – that she fell asleep and had a dream. She was looking out over the beautiful valley behind Pepperland. It was suffused with light that was pouring in from the far end, and against the light she saw two figures – mine, and that of Quintin Carr who had died a few months previously. He had been a close friend and spiritual adviser at the Hall, and we'd all known him as 'Grandpa'. In Sue's dream, the two of us were deep in conversation and obviously very relaxed and happy. When she woke, Sue realised she'd been given a foretaste of heaven and that whatever happened I was safe in the care of God. There was nothing she need worry about, and she was able to face the difficult days ahead in complete peace. Slowly, I regained my strength.

Soon after her dream, Susie came into the ward with a bunch of wild flowers in her hands.

'Aren't these lovely?' She held them over my head so I could see them. I was in traction and spent my time either looking at the ceiling or tipped up slightly to one side or the other to contemplate the upper part of the walls.

'Beautiful. Where did you find them?'

'Growing on a rubbish dump,' came the surprising answer.

Those flowers taught us something very significant. Sue told me how they had transformed what was an ugly mess of broken bottles and refuse, making the rubbish dump almost pretty. It seemed amazing that they'd grown in such unlikely soil, but this made us think of our situation. Our lives were broken as a result of the accident, and in many ways the future seemed bleak. I was almost completely paralysed from the neck down – what use could I ever be to God or to anyone else now? With the eye of faith, we saw that God could bring good even out of this – even if it was far ahead, even if we couldn't imagine what it could possibly be. He made flowers grow on a rubbish dump – what might He do for us?

For the first time, we allowed ourselves to hope and to be optimistic about the future.

There really wasn't time to brood at Stoke Mandeville.

Every waking moment was busily occupied, and the energies of staff and patients alike were concentrated on the goal of getting better – or at least making as much progress as was physically possible.

I don't think I've ever worked so hard as during my physiotherapy sessions.

'Come on, Max, you can do it. Move those fingers now.'

If it wasn't for the constant encouragement of my physio, I'd have given up long before my thumb seemed at last to respond to my efforts. Next, my fingers moved just slightly – then I could move my whole arm. I cannot describe the thrill of discovering that the paralysis would not be permanent after all. Once I realised the regular physiotherapy and exercise might mean the difference between making progress and perhaps being stuck in a wheel-chair, I entered into it with all my energy. No one said I would walk again. But I was determined to try.

I'd never been in hospital for any length of time before, and had no idea of the unique bond that could be built up between patients. Everyone is in the same position, whether he is old or young, rich or poor, and the only competition in our case was to see who would move up the ward the quickest to discharge and freedom. There was a cheerful camaraderie in our ward, 2X, and friendships developed that were among the most significant I'd ever known. I grew close to men whose paths I'd probably never have crossed in the normal course of events, and with whom I might have had little in common if it wasn't for our shared experience of neck and back injuries. We followed each other's progress, kept the ward's spirits up with jokes, sympathised with each other's drawbacks and disappointments. The key was acceptance. No one thought me unusual to be unable to do everyday, normal things like brush my teeth or write my name. And when I did progress to these things – after agonies of trial and error – I was cheered and congratulated as if I'd just scaled Everest. It felt like that sometimes, too.

Even my Christianity was accepted. If I'd thought about

it, I might have anticipated rude jokes or ridicule – or worse, a silent acknowledgment that there was no point of communication. But Tommy and Boyd and the others were very frank about what they thought of religion, and respected how much my faith meant to me. They joked about it at times, but always in good-humour, and sometimes they seriously wanted to know more. They were even sensitive about such issues as swearing – they apologised to me if they did it! God was very real in 2X during the time I was there, and I know I wasn't the only one who appreciated His presence.

By the time Christmas came, I had real cause for rejoicing: I'd taken some shaky steps with the help of the handrails in the physio department. I could also manage a quick shuffle supporting myself on someone's arm, but it needed to be a strong one so I could hold on for dear life!

It was my wheel-chair that really gave me mobility. What a joy it was to have a measure of independence again and to be able to propel myself around the ward and visit my friends. And to think I used to regard wheel-chairs as nothing but an encumbrance, the occupant an object of pity – now I knew better. Managing to sit up without falling over, staying conscious and not fainting, being able to move my arms enough to turn the wheels, managing to get in and out by myself – if very slowly and clumsily – all this was a triumph. And the amazing progress I'd made since being completely paralysed came home to me all the more when I looked around the ward. Some of the others would never move again, let alone manage a wheel-chair. I was richly blessed, and could only marvel.

But it would be different once I left the safety of 2X.

'They say I can come home for Christmas,' I told Susie excitedly, when the doctors had agreed I was well enough. 'For *ten days*.' I'd already been allowed home for a couple of weekends, but this seemed a real indication that I was much better. Soon, I thought excitedly, I should be able to go home for good.

I didn't think about the confusion and exhaustion I'd felt during those first couple of weekends with the family. They were just a shadowy memory, but within a few hours of arriving home again it all came sharply back into focus. Helplessness gripped me.

'They'd like us to go to the Hall for Christmas breakfast,' Sue's words rang in my ears. I'd agreed quite happily at the time from the security of my hospital bed, but suddenly I didn't want to go. I thought of telling Sue I couldn't face it, but the disappointment of all those who had been praying so sacrificially and faithfully for me was even more difficult to contemplate. I couldn't let them down. I steeled myself to brave it out.

We were a bit late. 'Have they already started?' I whispered anxiously to Sue. She was opening the dining-room door.

'No – don't worry. We're just in time, I think.'

It looked a long way to the other end of the room and our table. I clutched Sue's arm tightly. Please, Lord, don't let me fall over.

We began to walk across the wooden floor, and mentally I rehearsed all the advice of my physiotherapists as I put one foot in front of the other. Our footsteps echoed and my own were uneven because of my limp. The right side of my body was still largely paralysed, and it was only by swinging my leg from the hip that I could take a step at all. I frowned in concentration. Not too bad. They'd have been proud of me back in the ward.

Then I heard someone start to clap – and another and another. Before we were even halfway up the room, everyone was on their feet, clapping and cheering. It nearly proved fatal for my hard-won poise – I almost lost my balance!

But the ten days seemed endless. The prospect of them had been golden, but the reality was very different and almost more than I could bear. I was confronted with the seeming impossibility of ever getting back to normal living. My wheel-chair seemed hopelessly clumsy and stuck out like a sore thumb. It wouldn't go over the steps or up the stairs, it got stuck in doorways and took an endlessly long time to propel from one room to another. If Sue pushed me I felt doubly helpless and frustrated, and yet I needed her help desperately. I could do almost nothing without her, and the self-esteem that wasn't difficult to hold on to in Stoke Mandeville, where to be handicapped was to be normal, slipped out of my grasp like water.

I'd looked forward to it all so much, and especially to seeing the children, but their energy exhausted me and their laughter and noise made my head swim. However would I cope when they discharged me from Stoke once and for all?

It was an enormous relief to be back in the ward, and as soon as I got there, I wrote Susie a letter. I wanted badly to apologise for my crabbiness over Christmas. She'd worked hard to make it a very special ten days, and I'd done little but brood and vent my frustration in angry outbursts. When I'd finished, it looked like a drunken spider had fallen into an inkpot and made his escape across my clean sheet of notepaper. It had seemed an amazing achievement even to hold a pen, let alone write, but the results of my left-handed efforts seemed pitiful just then. I sent the letter none the less.

I went home for good about a month later. There was much celebration in the ward at my having 'made it', but I looked ahead with trepidation.

Six months is a long time to be away, I found myself thinking one afternoon. A pale, winter sun slanted through the kitchen window on to my motionless legs. They were thin and wasted. I moved the left one impatiently to thump my foot on the wheel-chair step, as if I was giving the thing a kick. Would I ever manage without the chair?

The children were romping about the house – they'd changed so much. I'd seen them in hospital on a few occasions once I was out of traction and wouldn't scare them by my appearance, but that was very different from being back in their world at home. I felt a stranger. Six months seemed like six years.

'Dad, do you want to see my new library book?' Nodi's voice broke into my thoughts. The nickname had originated in Africa when Jane found it impossible to pronounce Naomi and called the baby 'Nozi', and became Noddy – later amended to Nodi according to her own preference – when Anna failed to manage either of the other two versions. She was standing at the kitchen door, flourishing a large volume with a picture of a horse on the front. She loved horses.

'Yes, let's have a look.' I could manage that. I didn't have to move.

'Are you all right, Daddy?' Nodi said with her arm round my shoulder.

'I'm fine, love.'

At least the children didn't act as if they thought I was odd. They seemed to accept me as lovingly as if I'd never been away. Only Ben was rather puzzled by my presence, and I'd already seen him looking at me with his thumb in his mouth as if he was wondering who this person was who spent so much time sitting down. He'll get used to me, I thought, just like I'll get used to being home again.

'Max, it's so lovely to have you back,' Sue said frequently in the first few days. Sometimes I didn't believe her. I could see that she had managed beautifully while I'd been away and I felt a hindrance rather than anything else. I wanted to tell her that it was lovely to be back, but often the words stuck in my throat.

The first time she touched my hand in affection it went off into a spasm and I recoiled from the shock and confusion in her eyes. She tried to laugh about it – 'I must remember your right hand has a mind of its own' – but I felt utterly miserable. I couldn't make my body do what I wanted it to, and I couldn't stop it doing what I despaired of. Sue made many gentle efforts to restore our old closeness, but it was more than I could handle, and I just

137

retreated further into my shell.

I began to spend hours just sitting and thinking about Stoke Mandeville and all the fun we'd had in the ward. I sometimes longed to be back, away from all the painful adjustment to life at home. When Susie broke into my thoughts I reacted sharply and guiltily – unable to share what I'd been feeling. It would just cause her concern that I was still unsettled despite all her loving, caring efforts, and, anyway, she didn't really know what it had all been like. Yes, she'd met the lads and participated in all the activity of the ward when she came to visit at weekends, but it wasn't the same as being there day after day, and I felt she couldn't possibly appreciate the bond that had developed between us all.

One day, shut in my study, I painstakingly composed a letter to my old buddies and it cheered me up enormously. I made my pathetic efforts with the wheel-chair into a joke, and I could hear them laughing. Even in my imagination, that restored perspective.

'Max.' I heard Sue's voice and guiltily realised I'd been in the study for ages. The letter was finished long ago, and lay ready to be posted on the desk. I was pleased with the way I'd managed to fold it and put it in the envelope without crushing it.

'Coming, love,' and I propelled myself out of my cocoon of safety.

'We need some more logs for the fire so I'm just going down to the woodshed to chop a few – would you keep an eye on the children? They're painting in the kitchen.' She pulled on her anorak and added cheerfully, 'I'm quite practised at this now you know.'

I looked glumly after her. I always used to chop the logs, and would have to work really hard if I was ever going to do it again. But perhaps it was simply an impossibility. I didn't want to think about that.

Admiring the swirls of bright colours the children were happily dolloping on to large sheets of paper, I became painfully conscious of Sue's and my changed roles. She was doing almost all the things I would automatically have taken care of before, and instead of admiring the way she was coping I was resentful and unhappy. I despaired of having anything worth while to bring to our home and family, even to our relationship. It all came home to me once and for all when a fuse needed replacing in one of the kitchen plugs.

'Oh, I'll take care of that,' I assured Sue. 'Good physio for my hands.' If I can write with my left hand, I told myself, I can hold a screwdriver with it. Sue wisely left me to it, but what seemed like hours later I had to admit defeat.

'Susie, darling,' I tried not to sound as wretched as I felt. 'I can't quite get the fuse in after all.' She mended it in minutes.

It was the fact I couldn't be the husband I wanted to be for Susie that got me down the most in those early days. I knew that in many ways I had not done all that I should in our marriage, but at least I had maintained a standard of chivalry and care which I felt was very important. Now, I couldn't even open doors for Susie or help her on with her coat, never mind anything else. Being able to look after her in these little ways was symbolic of my protective responsibility towards her and recalled the fact that she had been given into my care by her father at our wedding. They'd become channels of my love for her, ways of telling her that I loved her. Without them, I felt destitute and once again it seemed that our love was threatened. Love-making wasn't the same either. Not that it actually led to sexual frustration, but rather to a sense of not living up to my image of manhood.

I didn't see that my pride was getting in the way again. There were other ways of expressing love and at that time I was in danger of mistaking the action for the motivation – despite Sue's efforts to reassure me.

'Don't you know I love you for who you are? I love *you*, *Max*.' She emphasised the words so I'd understand. 'It doesn't matter what you can or can't do.'

It took me a very long time to accept that, and even longer to come to terms with it. It was painful to realise how much of my self-image had been built on capabilities and achievements, and that I'd also been guilty of judging others by a similar yardstick. Once I'd really grasped that Sue meant what she said, and that I wasn't useless in the eyes of God no matter how I felt, I knew a reassurance and freedom deep inside that I had never experienced before. But layers of wrong attitudes and false securities had to be stripped away before I could come into a full realisation of my acceptability and start to live more confidently again.

Every day, I exhausted myself with the physiotherapy exercises I'd been given to do by my physio at Stoke Mandeville. I knew I had to keep them up just to maintain the level of movement I'd achieved so far, but my efforts were fuelled now with the determination to improve even more. I'd left Stoke with an unconscious optimism that with God's goodness and my hard work, I'd get back to normal. Only now was I beginning to realise this might not be the case, and I fought against it with all my might.

'Sue, I'm going to buy a car.'

I'd been home less than a month and I'd got thoroughly sick of having to be ferried everywhere by other people. I'd always disliked being a passenger in a car, anyway, and since the accident my intolerance of other people's driving had increased significantly. Sue was always very careful as she negotiated corners and bumps, but I had inevitably reached a pitch of frustration by the time we arrived at our destination. I'd got over my nervousness about travelling by car very quickly, and there seemed to be no ugly memories of the accident – so what was stopping me from driving again myself?

Sue could have said all sorts of things, of course. You can hardly walk, so how do you suppose you'll be able to drive a car? Your right leg is paralysed. You still can't control the spasms. You were nearly killed last time you drove . . . But she didn't raise any of these objections, just

140

quizzed me enough to know that my mind was firmly made up.

'I shall arrange to have a test drive, so don't worry, and I shan't spend the money if it's just going to be wasted,' I added, like a true Scot.

I needed a good car with comfortable seats to support my troublesome back – a Ford Granada seemed just the job. I'd never driven such a smooth, grand car before. This one was a stunning, metallic gold colour with soft velour seats. It was an automatic, and I had no trouble at all on the test drive.

'It went like a Rolls-Royce,' I told the seller. 'I'll have it.'

And it gave me a new lease of life – independence, mobility. I was quite unafraid, and could operate it without my handicap getting in the way. All the same, I eventually had it adapted so the accelerator pedal was on the other side and could be worked with my left foot which at least still moved even though I couldn't feel anything in it.

It was the children, alongside Sue, who helped me towards a new sense of identity and purpose.

'Daddy, sit down there and I'll tie your shoe-lace.' It was Annie, standing in front of me and pointing a stubby finger at the armchair in the corner of the kitchen. She'd been playing happily with her dolls'-house on the floor, and I'd been panting away at my walking practice. I looked down at my shoe and saw the trailing lace.

'Thank you, Annie.' I moved towards the chair. 'That's very kind of you.'

If an adult had suggested it, I would have been affronted. With great difficulty and plenty of time, I probably could have managed to tie the lace myself, but how could I refuse my own daughter?

I looked at Annie's blonde head as she fumbled with the lace and felt a rush of tenderness for her.

'Mummy says never to go round with loose laces 'cos you might trip up and hurt yourself,' she was saying. 'But it's difficult for a daddy with a wobbly hand, so I 'spect she'd let you off.'

The job done she jumped up, accepted my kiss of thanks and returned to the dolls'-house.

I marvelled again that she seemed to have accepted so completely and without difficulty my change of status at home. It didn't matter to her a bit that I couldn't do things I used to do. She didn't mind that I couldn't give her piggybacks any more, or race about playing energetic games. She and Nodi chatted away to me exactly as they had always done, and now that I had more time to listen I began to appreciate much more how they saw things and what made up their world. Although I didn't fully realise it at the time, the door was opening on to a whole new relationship with my children.

'Now, Nurse, how is our patient today?' Nodi had perched the frames of a pair of glasses on her nose to lend an air of authority.

'Very bad, I'm afraid, Doctor,' Annie reported, shaking her head. 'Very bad indeed. He'll have to lie quite still for a long time.'

Which, of course, I was very good at doing. Hospitals was a favourite game and the girls seemed to love diagnosing whole lists of horrific ailments to keep me lying on my back on the floor. Bandages would be wrapped round my arms and legs, and poor Ben would be reprimanded if he made a noise in the 'sick room'.

'It's my turn to be the doctor now, Nodi,' and a whole new series of instructions would be issued by the incoming boss.

Once I was promoted to doctor, but the girls told me I was hopeless and had better stick to being the patient. That was fine by me.

Ben was into brightly-coloured building bricks at that stage, and spent hours on the floor in quiet, busy contentment. When I first sprawled down there with him he kept looking up as if he expected me to disappear to do something else any minute.

'How's this, Ben?' I asked when I'd made what I thought was a rather impressive little tower.

He grinned at me, and put another brick on to his own creation – a long maze-like structure. He was soon passing me different coloured bricks to help me expand my repertoire.

Normally it would have been the other way round. I would probably have been helping him when he got stuck, or making suggestions as to what he might build. But now that I took time to notice, I saw that he had plenty of ideas of his own and didn't get stuck very often.

Susie wove in and out of me and the children with the Hoover, or to answer the telephone or to pop something in the oven. She never seemed to stand still and I appreciated as never before just how much time was needed to maintain a home and look after three children, not to mention a crotchety husband. Sue had never been one to let time go by unfilled, but to see all the tiny things that needed her attention was an eye-opener for me. I thought back to how Annie had tied my shoe-laces and the advice she'd learnt from her mother. I hadn't taught her that, nor could I recollect noticing when her laces came undone and needed tying so that she wouldn't fall over. Sue had done that – and a thousand and one things I might never know about. It wasn't just the stint in hospital that had prevented my watching the children grow up and seeing to their needs – I'd been an 'absent father' in so many ways long before the accident.

It began to feel good to be home again, but none the less there were times when I felt so frustrated and angry that I didn't know what to do with myself. A cloud of depression settled over everything and I wondered if I should ever be able to smile or laugh again. Sometimes it felt as if a coil was winding itself tighter and tighter inside me, so that the least touch would fling it wide and spring my hurt and anger out in a cruel lash at someone else.

It was like that when I threw the telephone directory at Nodi.

The children had been noisy all morning and I had long since wanted to retreat to the privacy of my study or the bedroom. Nodi had been particularly mischievous, and I can't think what she did to trigger my anger, but suddenly all self-control was gone. I couldn't move fast enough to catch her, and I couldn't give her the spank I thought she deserved, so I picked up the nearest object to hurl at her – a heavy telephone directory.

'Daddy!' It was a shout of fear and horror, and she threw up her arms in front of her face.

The minute it had left my hands I wanted to claw it back. I saw it suspended in the air and couldn't believe I'd thrown it. Nodi's wail cut me to the heart and I almost sobbed with relief when the directory fell harmlessly to the floor. I couldn't even throw any more, but never had I been so glad! Nodi was shaking uncontrollably and the tears just wouldn't stop. I had to hug and soothe her for a long time, and it was a wonder she let me.

I was horrified by what I'd done and couldn't forget it. I thought I was doomed to be the worst possible father that the children could ever have been landed with, and my hard-won new confidence was pulled from under my feet.

8

Bringing up children is anything but easy. In fact, it must be one of the most demanding jobs in the world.

I'd taken a ridiculously long time to come to this conclusion, lulled into a sense of false security by their relatively straightforward needs as babies and then Sue's efficiency as I dashed all over the place with my work. Suddenly being faced with their many, varied and persistent demands once I was home again after the accident gave me quite a jolt. It was as much because I hadn't done a lot of thinking about what sort of father they needed that I found myself at a loss, but while I loved the new closeness I'd found with all three children, my sense of helplessness was painfully aggravated by what I saw as my inability either to cope with them or to do them much good.

Mealtimes were a real test of my resources. Hunger or tiredness made the children particularly fractious, and it only needed one tiny provocation to spark off a fiery exchange or desolate tears. I needed all my energy to master my knife and fork and so had little left to cope with a noisy family. There were times when I couldn't take even their natural boisterousness, never mind the more high-pitched variety, and I was guilty more than once of shouting simply out of frustration. Their looks of bewildered dismay and hurt only made me feel worse.

When I managed to talk to Susie about all this, the burden of it seemed less heavy. I was beginning to make the mistake of thinking she didn't have any problems with the children's behaviour. I remember being very surprised when she told me how worried she used to get when one of the children didn't finish everything on the plate. 'Then I realised it was bound to happen and didn't matter much, anyway. They'll always put something in their mouths if they're hungry. It wasn't as if they were wasting away after all, but I used to get quite cross with them.'

'But you hardly ever get cross,' I remonstrated at this confession.

'Max, I do. I'm just as bad as you really – you just haven't noticed!'

I shook my head. Sue always seemed able calmly to cope with anything. It was one of the amazing qualities that had brought her through the dark months after the accident.

'The children are bound to be naughty,' she was saying. 'It's just a question of deciding how to deal with it. We can't expect them not to exasperate us from time to time.'

I thought about that. Of course it was true, never mind whether their father was in a wheel-chair. And I realised guiltily that part of the problem was that I'd got used to a life at Stoke Mandeville without any such interruptions and demands. Perhaps there was even a niggle of resentment towards the children that my relative privacy was now invaded. That had to be scotched. The issue at stake was how to deal with the present, not how to retrieve the past. Funny how an environment I should never have chosen, the hospital, could none the less provide me with such security that even now I was reluctant to part with it.

'So,' I said out loud to Sue, wanting very much to come alongside her in her efforts with the children. 'How do we tackle it, then, when they try our patience?'

And for the first time, we aired one or two concrete ideas.

'Ouch,' yelled Annie at supper not long afterwards. 'Stop kicking me.'

'You kicked me first,' returned Nodi sharply. 'I want my knife and fork. You've pinched them.'

'I have not. You said I could have them at tea 'cos I

haven't got any special ones like you.' Annie's protest was tearful, and Sue looked across the table at me with big, questioning eyes. Here we go – how should we deal with this one?

Nodi leaped up from her chair and stretched across the table to whip the knife and fork back.

'Hey, that's not fair.' Annie vainly tried to grab her sister's triumphant prize and then put her elbows on the table, cradled her head in her arms and began to howl.

'Now Nodi,' Sue interrupted. 'Did you promise Annie she could have your special cutlery tonight?'

Nodi then launched into a long explanation of the exact circumstances in which she had apparently tentatively offered the loan of her precious utensils, but explained that since Annie had kicked her under the table it was most unfair that she should now lend her knife and fork, anyway, she didn't see why Annie couldn't have some of her own...

'Well, I think you are both being very silly and you should say sorry to each other,' pronounced Sue, and began deftly popping boiled eggs into eggcups round the table.

Nodi looked furiously resistant. Annie was still hiccuping. Sue and I exchanged another glance – here's hoping!

'All right,' Nodi said, resigned. 'Here you are, Annie. You can have the silly cutlery.'

Sniff. 'Thank you,' and Annie brightened up at once.

'Come on, love,' I coaxed, 'you haven't said sorry.' Apologies were duly exchanged and Sue and I relaxed. We caught each other's eye and grinned. That hurdle had been safely negotiated – and together.

We began to talk about such situations when the children were safely in bed, exchanging thoughts about what we might or should have done. Trying to anticipate the trouble spots made it easier to react rationally and not to fly off the handle. And we laughed together about our naive expectations of the children – little sinners don't

become angels as soon as they hop out of the cradle! I
began to think about what it really meant to be a father.

I was learning that by my own efforts alone I could never
hope to be the father I wanted to be to my children. Just as
well Sue's around, I told myself, but while two heads may
be better than one we were still only ordinary human
beings and very likely to make mistakes. There would
probably be any number of situations where one or other
of us would be feeling tired or under the weather, and
might be provoked to an unfair or irrational response to
the children's behaviour. My own vulnerability during the
months of readjustment made this clear as never before,
and it was Annie who unwittingly reminded me of it.

We were sitting round the fireside in the sitting-room,
having a discussion about when Jesus might come back to
earth. It was our family prayer-time in the evening, and
the children were in their dressing-gowns ready for bed.

'Everyone in the whole world will see Him come, won't
they?' Nodi asked seriously.

'That's right.' When I went on to say we'd all be caught
up with Him in the heavens, Annie's eyes grew round.

'Ooh,' she breathed, 'that will be fun! Will we zoom out
of the window like Batman?'

In an attempt to rescue the subject from the wilds of the
children's imagination before they got too far, I told them
how we needed to be ready for His return.

'We shouldn't want Jesus to find us doing anything He
wouldn't like, would we?' I said warningly, hoping they
might aspire to new heights of good behaviour, but Annie
was quick to pick up the implications of this for me.

'Daddy, were you expecting Jesus might come when you
threw that telephone directory at Nodi?'

I was mortified. Annie wasn't consciously accusing me,
but I felt accused and could hardly find the words to
answer her. No. If Jesus had come back just then He would
have been very sad at what I'd done. It was wrong.

I used to think I could and should be a good example to
my children, but it was clear that sometimes I would fall

148

down terribly. If I was relying on just that to help them grow up to love the Lord, I'd be on a hiding to nothing. It's so obvious really, as is the difference God makes to the whole equation, but I took a long time to grasp it. For ages I went around under the cloud of that one particular failure, but eventually I realised it mattered far less than I'd thought. Not that the wrong was in any way diminished – just that God cared for the children, too, and could work not only alongside but sometimes through our mistakes.

We'd welcomed all three into the world as gifts from God, and although He'd very definitely given us responsibility for them, they were only on loan to us really. He had the ultimate responsibility, and we could entrust them to His care as we'd entrusted so many other things and people to Him.

I felt quite liberated when I'd thought it all through. It meant I needn't be afraid of admitting my weaknesses to the children, or of apologising to them when necessary. With God's grace, I would go on trying to be an example to them, but it wouldn't be the end of the world when I fell down.

It was almost a year since the accident and I'd reached a sort of plateau in my recovery. I was unlikely to regain any more movement down the right side of my body, which was still largely paralysed, and I'd only recovered a little of the feeling down my left side. I was a split personality – having what the medical profession termed Brown Sequard Syndrome. Regular exercise and physiotherapy were still vital if I was to maintain the level of mobility I'd already achieved, but I felt much better and much more in command of myself – almost restless in fact. So when Justyn began to show signs of exhaustion running the Hall single-handed, I saw little choice in the matter. He badly needed a break, having cut short his sabbatical to take up the reins again after my accident, and I decided it was time I went back.

'Max, you can't.' Sue's protest was forceful and adamant. 'It's far too soon and you know how much work you'd have on your plate. You simply must get your strength back completely before you get going again.'

'If I take it slowly, I should manage all right,' I reasoned. 'I've got to start sometime after all.' Then, seeing the genuine anxiety on her face and wondering if she was envisaging losing me all over again to the all-consuming mission of the Hall, I added gently, 'Don't worry. I won't overdo it this time.'

There was a bit of me that wanted to hide from facing the full-time demands of the world outside. I was still physically very weak and wasn't under any illusion about that, but at the same time I felt ready to take up the challenge of the Hall again. If I could rise to it, the accident would be well and truly behind me. It would be tangible evidence that I was back on my feet in every way.

'Why don't I just give it a try?' I said to Sue.

I knew I'd need help.

I was all too aware of the amount of time-consuming telephoning and letter-writing there would be, quite apart from running the conferences themselves and seeing that the outreach of the teams was organised effectively. I'd had a job to keep abreast of all the administration when I was working at full strength before the accident, so I knew I couldn't hope to manage when I was now so much slower and tired so easily. I risked being buried and stuck from the very start.

I must find a secretary, but it would need to be the right person – someone who could understand my frequent need to rest, and be willing to share the responsibilities I was taking on.

Penny. Her name popped into my mind and it was like an answer from heaven. Penny Burton had been a physiotherapist at Stoke Mandeville and as a Christian had quickly become a friend during my time there. Would she consider giving up her job to become my secretary?

'It would be wonderful,' Sue enthused. 'She would be

able to help you with your physio too. Do ask her. The Lord might have it all planned.'

And amazingly, Penny agreed. There was just one problem. 'I can't do shorthand!' she confessed over the phone.

I was so exhilarated that she could come at all that this seemed a very minor drawback.

'We'll send you on a course. Does it take long to learn?'

'Well, I don't know,' Penny was laughing. 'It'll put us on an equal footing, I suppose. I'll have to work at that and you can work at your physio.'

But even with Penny's efficient and considerable help, I was almost overwhelmed by everything that needed to be done at the Hall. The reality of my disability was brought home to me again and again as I stumbled over the corners of carpets and found myself longing to sit down and rest when I'd hardly been on my feet for any length of time. It was hopeless to try and manoeuvre the wheel-chair up and down the many steps at the Hall so I left it at home. How I longed for it sometimes! And how glad I was that Penny was used to people leaning on her arm for support. I looked to her more and more to take some of the strain I was under. I couldn't turn the clock back now and somehow we had to manage.

I kept thinking that I could slot back into my old groove, and that the other staff at the Hall needed me to do that, but the truth of the matter was that I simply couldn't. I didn't have the physical capacity, and was constantly brought up short by sheer exhaustion.

'Right,' Penny often said as I got slower and slower in my dictation. 'Time for you to go home.'

Sometimes I joked that in going I was just letting her catch up with her shorthand, but more often I was too tired to argue.

Invitations to speak still came pouring in, and although I schooled myself to turn many of them down, some were opportunities that I felt I couldn't pass by. It wasn't always the work at the Hall people wanted to hear about. Now, the word had spread about my accident and I was amazed at the way those who'd prayed for me or those who'd just heard what had happened wanted to hear how Sue and I had coped and what God had done for us.

Penny became my chauffeur as well as my secretary and physio. Many of these speaking engagements were a long way away and although I argued when it was first suggested that Penny help with the driving, I knew I would be too tired to speak let alone drive back again if I insisted on managing the journey myself. This was one of the concessions I was learning to make to my disability.

Without Penny, I don't know how I would have got through those difficult months. She was not only a tremendous support to me but became a fast friend of the whole family. Living near by it was easy for her to pop over, and she would often baby-sit for Sue and me – much to the delight of the children. The girls' enthusiasm for their recorder practice was boosted no end when Penny sat down on the floor beside them and proved herself a masterly player.

She fitted in so well with the family that I didn't notice what effect my reliance on her was having on my relationship with Sue. Without realising it, I was beginning to talk and share more with Penny than with my best friend, my wife. We spent hours together at the Hall and both grappled with its demands, so inevitably we talked and prayed things through. Sue was excluded from this, and once I was home I didn't want to think back over the problems of the day – especially if I felt they were already more or less sorted out because Penny and I had worked at them.

The other side of it was that Penny provided a link with Stoke Mandeville. She'd known me there, and represented its safe, secure world. I felt totally at ease in her company because I didn't have to pretend – she knew about my disability and understood how I felt. And because I was having to seem strong and capable in the eyes of other people, I needed all the more to let my real feelings out to someone. And that person was Penny.

But it should have been Sue.

She didn't say anything for a long time, then one day it came out.

'Max, I wish sometimes I could be the one who drives you to your speaking engagements instead of Penny. Then I'd get to talk to you.'

She was ironing and her face was flushed from the heat. Her hands moved efficiently and quickly.

'Susie . . .' I tried to rouse myself from the depths of a comfortable armchair.

'It doesn't seem fair that you have all that time to talk and there's none left for me.'

'Sue, darling,' I remonstrated. 'I do talk to you.'

'But hardly at all now,' Sue cried with a vehemence that pierced my heart. 'You are always so tired.'

I had a terrible sense of *déjà vu*. I'd been here before, and yet how many times had I told myself I would never again let work come before my family? But I felt locked into a situation that was beyond my control, since there was no one else to manage the Hall, and I didn't have the energy to cope with it any other way than I was already doing. It was as much as I could do just to keep going.

Sue took my silence to be a hurt one.

'I'm sorry, Max. I know it's hard at the Hall and Penny's the best thing that ever happened – but I miss you at home.'

From the bottom of my heart I tried to assure her that I wanted nothing more than to be at home with her too.

'Justyn's coming back soon,' was the one consolation I could find. 'Things are bound to get easier then.'

His return that spring was like the light at the end of the tunnel, and at last I could draw breath. He was full of enthusiasm for a Christian seminar he'd been to in the United States, run by Bill Gothard. When he saw how worn out Sue and I were, he urged us to go to the next one.

'It's just solid Bible teaching about relationships and work and Christian discipleship. It would do you the world of good.' Justyn had told us frankly of his recent struggle with depression, and this seminar had been quite a turning-point for him.

But America seemed a long way away when all I wanted to do was to be at home more, and apart from anything else I couldn't see how we'd manage to afford such a trip. I told Susie about it none the less, and her enthusiastic response made me think again.

'Max, it would be wonderful to get away and have time just to be together. Do let's try and go.'

Sue was right that we needed time to relax and talk more than anything else. The closeness we'd worked hard to establish after I came home from Stoke Mandeville had been steadily eroded again over the recent months, and I found myself thinking back to the extraordinary bond that had been between us immediately following the accident. We were at one then in a way we'd never been before, and had not rediscovered since. That had been a unique closeness, which helped us both through one of the most traumatic experiences we'd ever known. The impact of such a crisis must always be very decisive – either throwing people together or wrenching them apart, but Sue and I saw God's protective hand on us, too.

The foundation of our relationship was still His. Surely we could recapture that oneness?

To our amazement and delight, the Hildenborough Trust offered to sponsor the trip to the States – we could go. The prospect filled us with excitement. We wanted nothing more than to seek the Lord, His rest and His direction. And to reach out to each other again.

The following November we left the children with Justyn and Joy and set off for the first holiday we'd had on our own together since Nodi was born.

The North American countryside was bleak but bright with winter sunshine and Sue commented that it matched our moods. We were both weary and drained of resources, but our hearts were expectant and we drank in every challenge of the week-long seminar in Rochester, New

York. Our time was our own in the afternoons and we'd wrap up warmly and walk for as long as I had energy. We talked as if we hadn't seen each other for years.

The teaching applied so pertinently and directly to us that it brought us to tears at times. We were reminded one morning of the need to accept things we couldn't change, and I was deeply convicted about how I still hadn't come to terms with what the accident had done in my life.

'I thought I had,' I confessed to Susie, 'but I still wish I could run and be like everyone else.'

It was painful to admit that even after two years I was still struggling to be the person I thought I ought to be instead of accepting the person I was.

'Oh, but Max, you've come such a long way. We both have – don't be too hard on yourself,' Sue hugged me very tight at that moment.

Yes, but I knew that as long as I still held on to the past I would be prevented from moving on to the next step that the Lord might have planned for me. The depression that continued to dog me stemmed from this inner resistance I was sure. I longed to put it behind me and start afresh. I knew I'd go on missing my old body, but it was time to stop mourning it.

Another morning was devoted to relationships and the importance of keeping the channels of communication open. Sue and I knew a lot about that, but the particular emphasis was on being prepared to apologise when wrong had been done. We were asked to search our hearts then and there, and ask forgiveness of our respective husbands and wives if we needed to.

I thought back over the recent past and what stared me in the face was my behaviour towards Sue since my return from hospital. She had borne the brunt of my anger and frustration, and for the first time I realised the enormity of what she'd had to put up with. I didn't know where to start to ask her forgiveness.

'Max, it wasn't that bad.' Sue tried to protest even as she acknowledged how hard it had been sometimes. 'I forgave you for that long ago – we talked about it before.' But it was a wonderfully cleansing, restoring thing to bring past hurts and misunderstandings to each other so that no barrier could remain between us. The power of repentance and forgiveness was awesome, and brought a deep peace between us that we hadn't experienced for a long time.

It was then Sue told me more about her troubled reaction to Penny and our increasing closeness.

'I'd wave goodbye as you drove off on another speaking engagement and feel left out. Penny was obviously so efficient and such a support to you, whereas I seemed to be doing nothing. I was just staying at home and looking after the children.'

It had happened without our realising it. Quite innocently and understandably, I'd drawn close to someone who was a good friend to us both. It hadn't occurred to me that Sue would feel so excluded, and I saw with appalling clarity how easily marriages could be threatened by seemingly harmless relationships.

It wasn't that Sue didn't trust me, or suspected there was any danger of losing me to someone else, but she was deeply hurt that I was sharing my thoughts and feelings with someone else. I remembered her plea that we talk more together, and knew I had failed her.

'Perhaps I should have said something before,' Sue pondered. 'But I knew that you badly needed Penny's help at the Hall and I didn't want to interfere with that. I never stopped being grateful that God sent her just at the right time, and – and you were always my sun, moon and stars. They just went out rather a lot!'

We laughed together, and cried, too. Miraculously, there was no bitterness or anger as we talked. Neither of us was in any doubt of the love of the other or the mutual desire to draw ever closer. Our commitment to each other was total, and we sought to learn from our mistakes. Penny would go on being our friend – she was dear to us, and her help at the Hall would continue to be invaluable. But if Sue and I were to preserve our love in its fullness and strength, as we had always wanted to do, we needed to recommit ourselves to sharing everything with each other. 'The killer of love is creeping separateness,' Sheldon Vanauken wrote, and Sue and I could see how subtly that separateness could come about.

We praised God for our renewed closeness, and for the way He had preserved our relationship through so many ups and downs. We took a blissful week's holiday once the seminar was over, and came back to England refreshed and renewed, looking to the future with our heads held high.

9

The children were growing up.

Nodi was 10 now, and had straight brown hair that hung to her shoulders and freckles on her nose. She'd caught Sue's habit of wrinkling her nose in distaste when she didn't like something. Annie was growing her hair so she could sit on it, as she informed me seriously, and it was already over halfway down her back. She was dreamier than Nodi. Ben, at nearly 5, was full of young mischief and had a seemingly endless capacity for energetic activity.

Sue and I had spent a lot of our precious time in the States discussing how we could give the children the security and happiness we longed to see them enjoy. I saw more clearly than ever how it was crazy to leave family happiness to chance when there were so many pressures and tensions working against the family unit: from inside, with the ordinary weaknesses and failures of parents and children alike, and from outside, in a society where divorce was escalating and the family was low on the general priority list. It wasn't enough just to hope for the best, trusting that God and common sense would see us through. It had to be something more.

It was Peter Letchford, the new director at the Hall, who really inspired me to think more about making a conscious project of the family. Justyn and I had been visiting him at his home in the States to extend our invitation that he join the Hildenborough team, and his family struck me as quite exceptional. I didn't hear one row in all the three weeks I was there! I don't think I've ever spent time in a happier family: everyone got on like a house on fire and seemed to enjoy each other's company enormously.

'There's no secret, Max,' Peter told me modestly when I asked how he did it. 'But it hasn't happened by accident, either. Dorothy and I have spent a lot of time carefully and prayerfully planning our family life and how to bring up our kids. It's not an easy task, but let me assure you it's well worth it,' and he talked willingly and enthusiastically about his family for as long as I wanted to listen, such was his closeness to them and involvement in all they were doing. Here was a man living in a way I was convinced was right yet felt I had only glimpsed.

It was an answer to prayer when Peter agreed to move with his family to England to take over the running of the Hall. Ever since the death of Quintin Carr, the 'elder statesman' of the Hildenborough Trust, who had been such a support and mentor to us both and, indeed, to the rest of the team, we'd felt the need for an older and wiser spiritual adviser. We missed the wisdom and godly insight Quintin had so wonderfully provided. Peter was God's choice to fill that role once more, and with his arrival we felt the team was really on its feet again and heading purposefully in the right direction.

Peter had reminded me how quickly time could rob us of the opportunity to enjoy the children and to help them get the most out of life. I'd really only just begun to appreciate them as individuals in their own right, each with different needs and interests and characteristics. Being at home and able to spend time with them after the accident had done that for me. We were getting to know each other better all the time, and the more we did the more excited I became at the potential of even our very ordinary family. We could have a great time together. We could develop our relationships so that we weren't just comfortable with each other but close, supportive, best friends.

Heaven was home, wasn't it? That was where we were

all headed after all, and everyone talked about it as 'going home'. Home was where your heart was, where you were happy. Jesus surely wouldn't have told us that he was going to prepare a place for each of us in heaven if we couldn't appreciate how wonderful that really was. Heaven was a house with many rooms, and there was a special place for everyone. And that was home. Could our home be like that – at least a little? Could Sue and I offer the children a place where they felt they fitted and could be themselves; where they were loved and supported and safe; and where they were happy?

We had tried to offer that to each other from the very beginning of our relationship, and now that relationship had become the foundation of something more – a family. The children were part of us and we were linked inextricably to them. Everything we'd wanted for each other we wanted for them, too.

How were we going to do it?

'It's not an easy task,' Peter Letchford had said, and we'd already begun to appreciate that! But if God was interested in marriage He was interested in the families that resulted and we dared to believe that He was on our side. If heaven really was on our doorstep, we couldn't wait to let it in!

The starting-point, Sue and I agreed, was our own relationship. God had already strengthened and moulded it so much over the years, and we could see now that the benefits were not simply for the two of us to enjoy. With the children in our care, it was even more important that our relationship was secure and nourished by God. Planning was required here first and foremost.

'Right,' I decided categorically, after we'd talked all this over. 'No more relying on catching up with each other when we have a spare moment. We must keep a whole evening free every week just for the two of us.' That would have seemed an almost criminal indulgence before. 'We need it,' I continued, although Susie didn't seem about to lodge a protest, 'and we owe it to the children. Agreed?'

'Agreed.'

That was the easy bit. The hard bit was trying to bring our ideals down to earth and put them into practice.

It was lovely when the children willingly participated in our evening family prayer-times, but often they didn't. Of course it was understandable they would be sleepy, or hungry (only when they spied the fruit bowl), or remember there was a favourite television programme on just then, but when our efforts to interest them in a Bible story or reading from a Christian book failed miserably, we wondered whether it was worth the attempt. If the children were going to be put off Christianity by too rigorous a discipline at home, we'd surely be doing more harm than good.

Sometimes, indeed, the prayer-times just didn't happen. If it had been an exhausting process just getting the children into their pyjamas and nightdresses, or there was any kind of distracting crisis such as the dog refusing to sit quietly in the next room, there was clearly no point in going on.

But when things went right, and our efforts to make the prayer-time fun and relevant without being too demanding actually worked, we were encouraged beyond measure. The children surprised us time and again with their grasp of spiritual truths. Their prayers were often heartfelt – for their friends at school, for someone who was ill, or unhappy, or in response to a particular need of their own. Sometimes Jesus seemed to be sitting right there with us, so conscious were we all of His presence.

For a long time, Ben didn't feel like praying. He'd shake his tousled head when Sue or I asked him if he wanted to ask Jesus anything. When he did join in, he liked to pray for Daddy, and I never felt anything but touched and humbled by his halting requests for my well-being.

What was more, we saw the prayers answered – and this not only encouraged us to persevere but excited the children no end. Their young faith took a firm root in the goodness of God.

We knew the dangers of trying to impose a specific step

of Christian commitment on the children. If we made it an issue, it would put pressure on them to conform to our wishes and they might do it out of a childish desire to please. We knew we couldn't plant faith in our children, just prepare the ground as well as we could.

Ever since Sue and I were in Africa, our practice of giving thanks to God before each meal had taken on greater significance. The poverty around us had made us even more aware of how blessed we were to be able to enjoy three meals a day, and we wanted the children to appreciate this, too. So, various ways of saying grace evolved around the kitchen table – some more thankful than others! Singing our thanks turned out to be the most popular way of doing it as far as the children were concerned, but I was very glad Nodi didn't choose that particular method when she and I were guests of the parents of one of our helpers at the Hall.

'Now do make a start,' Mrs Parker said, indicating the mounds of sandwiches and cake spread out on the table. 'Which kind of sandwich would you like, Naomi dear?'

Nodi was still very young and didn't hesitate in her reply.

'I can't start yet 'cos I haven't said grace.'

There was a stunned silence.

'Daddy.' Nodi turned to me confidentially. 'They haven't said grace.'

Giving her a knowing smile and feeling rather sorry for Mrs Parker, I whispered back, 'Yes, why don't you thank Jesus for your tea.' I had rather hoped she would do this quietly to herself, but with eyes closed and hands clasped tightly in front of her, she said, 'Thank you, Jesus, for my nice tea. Amen.'

By this time Mrs Parker was offering her husband an egg sandwich. Ready now to start, Nodi was soon tucking into one herself, quite unaware of the effect she'd had on the tea table.

Disciplining the children tested our resources enormously. It was very difficult to decide what to do when, and to know how severely to reprimand bad behaviour. And yet we knew we had to sort this one out. Discipline was the framework for security, and for learning right from wrong.

'Max, I just can't spank Ben,' Sue pleaded when he had done something we both knew deserved punishment.

I saw no choice. Ben needed to learn a lesson and there was no getting round it.

'Susie, you must. It's important.'

She shook her head miserably.

'Well, I can't do it any more, so it's got to be you.' I told her. My useless right hand meant I could no longer handle this particular problem as I would normally have done. Sue had never spanked one of the children before, but when she steeled herself to do it the punishment was doubly effective because Ben had never been disciplined by his mother like that. The seriousness of what he'd done came home to him all the more forcefully.

'Do you know why we had to spank you, Ben?' I asked him gently, later. It became a regular practice if we thought there was any danger of hurt or misunderstanding to talk to the children about their 'crime' in my study.

'Yes,' came the reply in a very small, tear-stained voice.

I explained again without further reprimand. 'And now it's finished,' I told him. 'It's in the past and forgotten.' I was so anxious for him to understand that. If even for a moment he thought he had failed us or could no longer count on our love, one wrong would only have been substituted for another. Forgive and forget had to become a practical reality.

We gradually worked out a scale of discipline, which was helpful because it gave us boundary lines as well as the children. It also meant that Sue and I would stand a reasonable chance of being consistent in our reactions to the children's behaviour, thus hopefully sparing them confusion. From close quarters, it wasn't always obvious that our efforts were achieving the desired results, and it was only as time went on that we could see positive development – or otherwise.

Forgetfulness was something we wanted to be vigilant about, but this was one area where we often had to curb our own impatience or irritation. Ben, for instance, was prone to forget to brush his teeth.

'Have you done your teeth, Ben?' Sue asked regularly after breakfast before he raced off to school or to play in the garden. He usually nodded, but when prompted with a further 'Can you remember having done them?' he wasn't so sure. 'Uum – I'll just go off and do them, shall I?'

We knew we had to distinguish forgetfulness from disobedience when it came to responding appropriately.

'We can't always tell, though,' Sue commented when we discussed this. That was true enough, but we found that if we observed and got to know our children well we could see clearly the difference between behaviour that merited punishment and that which just tried our patience. Equally, we discovered we couldn't just have particular punishments for particular wrong-doings since what mattered to one child and would bring the lesson home might be lost on another. For Nodi, it was a real deprivation to be denied her sweet after lunch on Saturday (when sweets were allowed), but Annie didn't like sweets much so a more effective action when she'd been naughty was to tell her she couldn't have an apple today.

'How can we really, day after day, show them how much we love them?' Sue and I asked ourselves. We came up with lots of ideas, but really to get to the bottom of it we focused our thoughts on how God loves us.

'Unconditionally.'

We wanted to try and reflect God's love in our love for the children.

We held on as well as we could to our one night a week together, and used it to discuss and pray about all that was happening with the children. We talked about a lot of other things besides and, eventually, as we began really to live and breathe and not just plan our family happiness, we didn't need to set a specific time aside because such discussion became quite natural to our normal, everyday conversation. Not that we stopped giving priority time to each other: we were achieving that at last in a natural, unstructured way.

The first time Ben knocked Nodi's paint water over, said sorry straightaway and trotted to get a cloth, Sue and I could hardly believe it.

'Ben, thank you,' Sue said at once. 'That was very good to apologise so quickly, and very kind to get a cloth.'

Ben grew an inch and Sue and I learnt that we had to 'catch them being good' as well as pull them up when they were naughty.

We wrote 'fun' into our emerging plan for family happiness as often as we could: picnic breakfasts, games evenings, candle-light meals, perhaps because it was the end of term or just the beginning of the weekend.

Birthdays were always special days of celebration.

'Move up, Dad.' I suspected it was very early indeed as two little people bounded on to Sue's and my bed and told us to hurry and wake up because it was Annie's birthday.

'Happy Birthday to you,' we sang at the tops of our voices when Annie joined us and opened her eyes wide in amazement at all the presents we'd piled on to the eiderdown.

'What's this – it's such a funny shape?' We all tried to guess and Ben giggled knowingly because it was his present. Annie savoured the present-opening as long as possible – appreciating the wrapping and ribbons as much as the gifts inside. We all offered our comments and admiration, and when the very last one was opened we rushed off downstairs to prepare the birthday breakfast.

Eggs with hats and cheese to sprinkle on was Annie's favourite, with rolls warm from the oven. Nodi went out to pick flowers from the garden to put round the birthday girl's plate, and Ben carefully arranged the cards the postman had brought for her to open.

Annie wanted a special party for this birthday, so we'd

arranged a barbecue in the garden. Everything seemed fine and, apart from dropping the sausages into the fire, the children were having a whale of a time.

'Mum, can we have the cake now?' Annie knew Sue had been cooking something special, but someone else had been at work. When Sue went to the kitchen to get the beautifully decorated strawberry cake, all she found was a few chewed-up candles and a very full dog who had taken her revenge at being shut away from all the fun.

That autumn, a year after our holiday in the States, Penny asked me if I would give her away in marriage to John Donaldson. Her father was no longer alive and the rest of her family were in Australia. 'You and Sue are the nearest to family I've got over here,' she explained, 'and I wondered if the girls could be bridesmaids, too.'

It was a compliment and an honour, and I accepted the invitation gladly.

'Get in some walking practice, mind you,' she warned finally. 'We don't want you tripping in the aisle.'

I realised how much I would miss this good-natured cajoling to keep up the physio, and how much I owed Penny for having come this far. I hardly ever used the wheel-chair now. Very occasionally in the evenings when my back ached and I was really tired, I'd get it out, and sometimes it went with us in the car if there was a longish walk at our destination – but I never liked to capitulate to it even then. It had been a security when I first came out of Stoke Mandeville and a great help, but now it was just an uncomfortable reminder of my disability. Penny had always told me there must come a point when I left it completely behind and thought positively about not needing to use it, and I had reached that point. None the less I couldn't quite bring myself to send it back – it went up in the loft.

God's timing is perfect, I reflected later when I thought about losing Penny's help at the Hall. Peter was safely installed as well as a new business manager, and things were running at a much more manageable pace. I was also able to organise my share of the work so that I could be at home a good deal more. Penny's philosophy as a physio was to work herself out of a job, and the Lord had worked her out of one at the Hall, too.

Before she left, Penny had a final brain-wave.

'Why don't you try ski-bobbing on the skiing holiday this year?' Every year the Hall organised a skiing party to one of the many beautiful mountain resorts of Europe, and since skiing had been one of my favourite sports before the accident I hadn't relished the thought of leading the planned trip in the New Year and having to forfeit the exhilaration of plunging down the slopes.

I couldn't believe Penny was serious. Ski-bobbing was like skiing sitting down, or driving a motor-bike without wheels or engine, but fixed on to skis instead.

'Do you really think I could manage it?' I could imagine how fast those things went once they got going.

'If you keep up your exercises,' Penny replied characteristically.

I was as excited as a child and bought a bright red skiing hat with a pompom on top to celebrate.

Penny worked out some special exercises to help me strengthen the right muscles for ski-bobbing. The ski-bob itself sits on two skis, with the smaller one in front steered by the handlebars. The rider wears ski-boots and mini skis which extend two or three inches beyond the toe of the boot, enabling both balance and braking. Leaning cleverly from side to side when swooshing down a steep slope edges the skis into the snow for a better grip, and Penny devised games so that I could master this technique in advance. She made me dodge about the room without falling, so strengthening my toe, foot and ankle muscles as well as giving me some practice in staying upright while swaying my body from side to side.

'Just don't go breaking your leg,' Sue warned before I left. 'Either of them.'

The holiday was a roaring success. I had the time of my life, shooting past the guests on my snow machine and discovering that being partially paralysed didn't have to be restricting at all. I may not be able to ski like I used to, but I wasn't at all sure that ski-bobbing wasn't more fun!

In years to come, the whole family would enjoy skiing together, fulfilling a dream I thought would be denied me for ever. My hopes of bringing up my children on lots of healthy and energetic outdoor holidays had been well and truly dashed by the accident, but the seemingly impossible was not beyond our gracious heavenly Father.

One of the many things for which we thanked God after the accident was the way the children had been protected from trauma. Everyone had been amazingly kind and concerned to help when Sue was coming over to Stoke Mandeville at the weekends, and the children seemed to survive the whole unsettled experience extraordinarily well.

But then Ben began to worry us. He was more and more out of sorts and crotchety at home, and seemed to have lost interest in so many things.

'Perhaps it's just a phase,' we thought, and tried to wait patiently for him to go through it, but nothing seemed to improve. He insisted he was fine when we asked him, but his listlessness spoke for itself. Was Ben scarred in a way we hadn't realised?

'Max, have you noticed Ben isn't doing his reading at all?' Sue asked worriedly after tea one evening. His school-book lay unopened on the table with its marker carefully in place. 'He's supposed to read a bit every day.'

I asked him about it.

'Oh!' Ben looked puzzled. 'Yes, it's about farms. I like it.'

'Have you nearly finished it?'

Ben thought for a moment. 'I haven't read much lately,' he said. Although I tried to encourage him, I noticed the marker stayed near the beginning for days.

Ben attended the same primary school that the girls had hugely enjoyed but, once we realised his problem might stem from there, we thought about moving him to a different school. The large classes clearly didn't suit him, and since there was no other state school near by which could offer the more disciplined approach we felt Ben needed, we considered private education. Each child needed us to respond individually to his or her needs, and we felt this was right for Ben.

We could only act in faith, hoping and praying the change would mark a turning-point. Ben was very pleased with his new uniform.

'Dad, we had football and we go swimming tomorrow and the boy sitting next to me lent me his new pen – look!' We waited for the first flush of excitement to wear off, but it didn't. Ben's new environment was just what he needed and we breathed a sigh of relief.

The girls loved school and always had some funny incident to relate when they came home. Very often they came out with some surprising questions.

'Mum,' Nodi asked seriously one teatime. 'Did Henry the Eighth really start the Church of England?'

Sue's 'yes' didn't satisfy Nodi.

'But he had lots of wives,' she remonstrated.

'Well – yes, he did.'

'He was a bad man, then, so how could he have started the Church of England?'

So a discussion began which took up most of the meal. It seemed that the history teacher had told the children about the Reformation as if it was all quite acceptable and straightforward. Nodi was baffled that no comment had been offered on old Henry's behaviour when she knew from what we'd taught her at home and what she'd learnt in church that he was hardly doing the right thing in getting rid of so many wives!

No matter how much we would have liked to have an answer to every problem before it came up, that could only ever be wishful thinking. The reality of life at Pepperland was very different, but at the same time there was an increasing closeness between us as we all mucked in. Or so I liked to think. We *did* have good times together – lots of them, and if nothing else could be chalked up after these first few years of making a real priority of the family, we were definitely a new and stronger unity. It wasn't us and the children any more. It was just us – all of us. 'Children add a new dimension,' Sue's father had said, and I thought I now knew what he meant. The dimension was simply there and Sue and I were part of it – swept along in it and loving it, for all the inevitable headaches and heartaches. I could no longer imagine what life would be like without the children.

As the children got older, Sue felt freer to contemplate taking on some of the things she'd been itching to get back into, and an opportunity came up at the primary school for her to run the lunch-time Christian Union meeting.

We knew it would be no light commitment, and I was concerned at first that she might not be able to do it real justice since her time was already very full.

'Well,' Sue reasoned, 'it would be great fun as well as a help. And wouldn't it be good to get to know the teachers better and some of Annie's friends and their parents? I think it could be quite important.'

She was already excited at the prospect, and we agreed that she should give it a go. In the end she ran the Discovery Club for two years until Annie moved on from the school. The highlight of that time was the school assembly Sue was invited to take, when she was showered with compliments from amazed parents and teachers who said she'd obviously livened up the group no end. 'They couldn't believe how meaningful the Bible was to the children,' Sue told me.

Wherever there was an opportunity to encourage and support the teachers of our children, we tried to take it. Many of them did a marvellous job, but we wondered how many parents ever said so. We aimed to remember them at Christmas with cards and greetings, and when the children changed forms we sent letters to the teachers thanking them for what they had done during the year. And we prayed for them regularly. It took a while before we felt courageous enough actually to tell them this, but eventually we did. In order to discipline ourselves to remember them in prayer, Sue and I made a point of bringing them before God on our way to and from the schools with our car-loads of children. That way one or other of us would certainly be praying for them daily, as we did for the children at the same time.

One day I made an important decision.

'It's time to send the wheel-chair back to Stoke Mandeville.'

'Oh no,' piped up a dissenting voice. 'Can't I have rides in it any more?' Ben looked aggrieved.

It had been up in the loft so he hadn't actually played with it for a long time.

'You've grown out of it now, Ben,' I told him. 'Just like I have.'

'But Dad, you *might* need it again you know,' Nodi said. 'When you get tired.'

'But I can sit in an ordinary chair.' Now that I'd envisaged cutting the tie to Stoke Mandeville and those months of incapacity once and for all, I couldn't wait actually to do it.

The postman came for it a few days later – 'Will we have to wrap it up in brown paper?' Ben had asked – and we all watched him put the chair in his red van and drive away. Another chapter was closed, but in fact it felt as if it closed a long time ago. I had moved on and the chair didn't belong any more.

Who could possibly have believed when I was lying paralysed in hospital that one day I would be able to walk and cycle and even ride with my children. Cycling was one of our favourite activities and once I'd mastered the balance I usually managed quite well – but not always.

'Dad,' Ben yelled, just as we'd started off up the drive on one expedition. 'My chain's come off.'

'Right,' and I concentrated on cycling up beside him. If I was going to stay upright when I stopped the bike, I had

171

to put my good foot down, but somehow I got confused and realised quickly that I was about to suffer a serious indignity.

'Woo-aah,' I yelled impressively as I keeled over towards the bluebells. With a loud crash, I acknowledged my failure to help my son in his distress.

'Dad!' Ben looked worriedly down at the collapsed figure of his father.

'Dad's fallen over,' he shouted unnecessarily to the others, who came hurrying back along the drive.

The whole thing suddenly struck me as enormously funny and I laughed even more when I saw Ben's surprised look. His expression wavered, and then he joined in with obvious relief.

'C'mon, Dad,' Nodi giggled, and tried to pull me up. 'You are silly. Have you hurt yourself?'

Afterwards I thought how amazing it was that I'd laughed instead of being furiously angry. At one time I would have suffered agonies of embarrassment and hurt pride, but now Dad's occasional mishaps were all part of the fun of the family.

How I'd changed! I laughed at myself. It was a sobering thought that if it wasn't for the accident I might never have discovered the richness of being an active family member – or at least taken longer to make the discovery.

'Do you know, Sue,' I found myself saying after we'd all come in, breathless from our cycle-ride. 'I think the accident was the best thing that ever happened to us.'

I was pretty staggered that I could make such a statement, but I really meant it. I recalled the 'rubbish dump flowers' and saw afresh that God had indeed brought a great deal of good out of a terrible situation. Our relationship and family had been immeasurably enriched.

'Will I still be the same age in heaven?' Annie asked not long afterwards, when we were on the way home from school. 'I mean, if Jesus came back today and I go to heaven, will I go on growing up? I don't really want to grow up. I'd just like to stay being me.'

Why is it that the children always ask such complicated questions when my Bible commentary is not to hand?

'Annie, in heaven you will be your very own self, but also like Jesus because the Bible says when we see Jesus we'll be like Him.'

'Will you still be my daddy in heaven?'

I was stumped by that one.

'Will we still be together as a family?' her anxious voice persisted.

'Well,' I said carefully, 'lots of things in heaven will be a bit like here only much, much better. Things that are good here are often spoiled by things going wrong, aren't they?'

'Yes, I suppose so,' mused Annie. She spoke her thoughts freely, and in earnest. 'I like being in our family so I was thinking it would be great if it could go on in heaven. But it would be a bit unfair for some of my friends like Jane whose Mummy left and now she's really sad.'

So that was it. She was as concerned for her friend as she was to find out what would happen to her. Perhaps, too, she was a little afraid, in a deep, unacknowledged part of herself, that our family might not always be together, so I quickly tried to reassure her.

It delighted me that Annie hoped heaven would be like home. She'd touched on the very thing that Sue and I had hoped, wondered and prayed about. God in His graciousness was giving us a little bit of heaven on our own doorstep, in amongst the fairly chaotic daily life of Pepperland.

How truly wonderful it will be when we reach the special place He's prepared for His people – for all of us.